Ever after high

EVER AFTER
Royals!

Fairy Tail

Ending

A SCHOOL STORY

Suzanne Selfors

LITTLE, BROWN BOOKS FOR YOUNG READERS
www.lbkids.co.uk

This book is dedicated to Kara Sargent, for being my compass and friend as we made our way through magical waters. Thank you.

LITTLE, BROWN BOOKS FOR YOUNG READERS

First published in the US in 2016 by Little, Brown and Company
First published in Great Britain in 2016 by Hodder and Stoughton

1 3 5 7 9 10 8 6 4 2

A CIP catalogue record for this book
is available from the British Library.

ISBN 978-1-51020-030-2

Printed and bound by CPI Group (UK) Ltd, Croydon CR0 4YY

The paper and board used in this book are
made from wood from responsible sources.

MIX
Paper from
responsible sources
FSC® C104740
www.fsc.org

Little, Brown Books for Young Readers
An imprint of
Hachette Children's Group
Part of Hodder and Stoughton
Carmelite House
50 Victoria Embankment
London EC4Y 0DZ

An Hachette UK Company
www.hachette.co.uk

www.hachettechildrens.co.uk

Contents

A Magic

Wind

he view from the ship's bow was breathtaking. In the east and in the west, a calm turquoise sea stretched to the horizon, the perfect flatness interrupted only by diving seagulls and dancing porpoises. But to the south, which was the ship's direction, the sea met an expanse of jagged white cliffs. Tall trees grew atop the cliffs, forming a dense forest. And rising above the forest, as if trying to touch the cloud-dappled sky, were the turreted towers of Ever After High.

For students who arrived by boat, this first glimpse of the school was a welcoming beacon. To know that the sea journey was about to end was a relief to many. And to know that a new year was about to begin, in the most famous and most prestigious school in all the fairytale lands, induced shivers of excitement. But on this particular day, the girl standing on the bow felt neither relief nor excitement.

Meeshell gripped the railing so tightly her knuckles turned white. She held her breath for so long, she nearly turned blue. There it was. Her school. Her future.

Her story.

Like many before her, Meeshell had traveled from a faraway kingdom. But hers was a land that most had never seen and would never see. It was shrouded deeply in mystery. A place of fable. A place of unequaled beauty. A place nearly impossible to reach, unless one had the correct physical attributes.

She might as well have come from the moon, for

that is how strange her world would seem to her fellow students.

She didn't, however, come from the moon.

She exhaled, then shifted her weight. She'd been standing so stiffly, her knees had begun to ache. *Knees*, she thought. *Such weird, knobby things. Will I ever get used to them?* She reached down and gave them each a good rub, then returned her focus to the distant turrets.

"There is no better education than the one you'll receive at Ever After High," her father had assured.

"You'll learn much more than we could ever teach you," her mother had said.

"You'll do great!"

"You'll be fine!"

"You'll fit right in."

Ever After High was her father's alma mater, so it made sense that he was super enthusiastic about his daughter attending the same school. And her mother wanted the very best for her children, so she was excited, too. But Meeshell's heart ached from

leaving family and friends behind. And doubts churned. What if she couldn't figure out how to adapt to this new world? What if she didn't understand their strange traditions? What if she stood out, like a crab in a bed of starfish?

As the ship slid gracefully through the water, Meeshell closed her eyes and held her face up to the cool breeze. She liked the way it felt as it tickled through her long, pink hair. The breeze was too gentle to fill the ship's sails, but she'd remedied that little problem. Using her magic touch, she'd created a little wave and had aimed it at the boat's stern. The wave never crested; rather, it continued to push them along. The ship's captain had been grateful for her help. The narwhal he usually employed to pull the ship on calm, windless days was on vacation.

"Lass?" A man's voice interrupted the silence. Meeshell's eyes flew open. Captain Greenbeard stood beside her. "You want one of the crew to fetch your coat? You'll be catching a chill out here."

She shook her head. Cold air didn't pierce her, as

it did others. Besides, she didn't own a coat. They didn't have coats where she came from. It had been difficult enough finding a dress. Luckily, her mother had a vast collection of objects that had fallen from ships, or had been stolen off of beaches by rouge waves. Those objects included the plain yellow dress that fell to Meeshell's ankles, the white ribbon tied around her waist, and the bag that now contained her few precious belongings.

"You're certainly a quiet one." The captain leaned his elbows on the railing and stared straight ahead, toward the white cliffs. He was a rugged-looking fellow, with deep lines around his eyes and mouth. He'd been kind to her during the voyage, as had the rest of the crew. "I'm finding it difficult to believe you've never been on a ship before. Never?"

She shook her head again.

"Well, you handled yesterday's choppy weather like a true sailor. Didn't turn green or get sick. Takes most landlubbers weeks to get their sea legs."

Sea legs? She didn't know what that meant. She'd

gotten her legs three days ago and they were supposed to be for land use. Were there special legs for
the sea?

The captain glanced at a purplish bruise that
glowed on Meeshell's forearm. "All that stumbling
you've been doing, all that bumping into things,
that's to be expected. The ocean swells can be as
unpredictable as Poseidon's moods."

The captain was right. She'd certainly been struggling to walk gracefully. Because she'd been stuck on
a ship since getting her legs, she'd had little chance
to learn how to use them, other than walking up
and down the deck, or up and down ladders. The
physical bruises would go away. But what about the
bruises to her confidence? Only time would tell.

Though only three days had passed, the journey
from her kingdom had felt like eons. Too shy to talk
to the crew, and too distracted to focus on a good
book, Meeshell had tried to make the hours pass
faster by watching for sea creatures. But alas, no
matter how many pods of dolphins or seals she

spotted, time moved as slowly as a sea slug. Fortunately, her mother had packed her favorite foods. "It will take you a while to get used to what they eat on land," she'd told Meeshell. So, while the rest of the crew munched on salty smoked herring and dry cornmeal biscuits, Meeshell ate seaweed-and-kelp-berry salads.

"Never seen that kind of food before," the cook had commented with a shrug. He was a troll, with huge ears and a nose to match. "You should try my fish chowder." He shoved a bowl right up to Meeshell's nose. She grimaced at the sight of the fish tails and fins floating in the creamy stew.

"No, thank you," she politely told him. Her voice came out quieter than she'd intended.

"What's that you say?" he asked.

She cleared her throat. "No, thank you." It was very difficult to get the words out, not just because of her shyness, but because something was different about her voice. No matter how hard she pushed the words, they still came out quiet. Hopefully it was just a temporary ailment, and her voice would be back to normal before classes began.

"She said no, thank you," one of the crew told the cook.

"No fish chowder? But my chowder is famous."

"Famous for its aftereffects," another crew member said with a snicker.

The cook dismissed Meeshell with a wave. "Suit yerself." Then he scratched his rump with his wooden spoon.

Meeshell had eaten the last of her salad that very morning, and she'd been worried that she'd have to eat some of the cook's food. But now, with Ever After High in sight, there'd be no reason to risk an upset stomach. Fish was not on her menu. Never!

The white cliffs and stone towers loomed closer. "Land ho!" Captain Greenbeard hollered. Commotion arose on deck. Crewmen and women streamed out of the galley, wiping crumbs from their beards,

braids, and shirts. Captain Greenbeard took his place next to the ship's wheel. As the ship sailed around an outcropping, a quaint harbor came into view. A few smaller boats were moored at a dock that jutted out from a white beach. The sand sparkled, as if made from glitter.

"Drop the main!" the captain ordered. A large rope was untied and the billowy sail, with its narwhal emblem, collapsed onto the deck. Without any wind, it must have been some kind of magic that had held the sail aloft. The magic wave that Meeshell had summoned was no longer needed, so she waved it away.

Captain Greenbeard gripped the wheel as the ship glided toward the dock. "Man the lines! Rudder hard over!"

Meeshell stepped aside as a crewman grabbed the bowline. As the ship neared the dock, three crewmen jumped onto the rough planks, ropes in hand, then guided the ship to a standstill.

A sign stood at the end of the dock:

WELCOME TO STORYBOOK HARBOR
THIS WAY TO MIRROR BEACH

THIS WAY TO
EVER AFTER HIGH

Meeshell took a long, steadying breath. She'd arrived.

One journey had ended, but another was about to begin.

Fairest

Feet

The gangplank was lowered. Captain Green-beard picked up Meeshell's bag, then, with a flourish of his hand, said, "After you, lass."

The crew stood at attention, waiting for their only passenger to disembark. All eyes were on Meeshell. Did they suspect her true identity? If so, were they waiting to see if she could navigate that narrow piece of wood, or if she'd stumble and fall into the water? That would be quite a scene, and one she wanted to avoid!

"Thank you for the ride," she said to the crew, trying to be heard above the shrieking of a pair of seagulls, who'd swooped onto the deck to pilfer whatever crumbs they could find. Meeshell took a few steps forward. Then, ever so slowly, she made her way down the plank, telling herself to place one foot in front of the other. She didn't take her eyes off her new feet. The captain walked behind her.

"You're unsteady because you've been at sea," he told her. "You'll get used to land again in no time." She was glad to know that he still didn't suspect the true reason why she was unsteady, and she certainly hoped she'd quickly get used to land.

Upon reaching the dock, she sighed with relief. The dock was solid and steady, no movement from the waves. She pressed her toes against the wood and found her balance. Then the captain hollered, "Hello!"

A gentleman was walking down the dock. He appeared to be a dapper fellow, wearing a crisp black suit, a striped waistcoat, and a tie. His thick gray

hair and mustache were embellished with white streaks. A heavy key ring hung from his belt. Upon reaching her, he extended his arm. "You must be Ms....Ms...." He hesitated. "Ms. Meeshell." She nodded and shook his hand. "I am Headmaster Grimm. Welcome to Ever After High. I hope your journey was uneventful."

Uneventful? She wouldn't have chosen that word to describe what she'd been through over the past three days. Having never left home before, having never traveled alone, the journey had been the biggest event of her life! The headmaster must have noticed her confusion at his comment for he added, "No *major* events. Storms. Shipwreck. Giant squid attacks, that sort of thing. In other words, you appear to have made it in one piece."

She nodded again.

"We did get a touch of bad weather, but the wee lass fared well," Captain Greenbeard said.

"That does not surprise me." The headmaster gave Meeshell a knowing look. Then he glanced around. "Do you have luggage?" He glanced down at her feet. Her bare toes peeked out from under the dress's hem. "A pair of shoes, perhaps?"

"She travels light. Just herself and this bag." The captain handed it to the headmaster. "She's a quiet one. Only a sentence here or there, during the whole trip."

Headmaster Grimm took a small velvet pouch from his waistcoat pocket and handed it to the captain. "Thank you for your service," he said.

"Yes, thank you," Meeshell said, smiling shyly.

"You're very welcome." He took off his blue knit cap and bowed like a gentleman.

"Good-bye!" the crew called. Meeshell waved. Captain Greenbeard strode back onto his ship and ordered his crew to get underway. The gangplank was raised. Meeshell wondered if she should use her magic touch again, and give them a friendly push, but a gray head and long twisted horn poked out of the water, next to the boat. The captain's narwhal had returned.

"Follow me," the headmaster said.

As the narwhal pulled the ship from the harbor, Meeshell followed the headmaster up the dock. The boards were not evenly spaced, and some were thicker than others. She winced as a sharp pain pierced the big toe on her new left foot. "Ow."

The headmaster took her arm and led her to a log. She sat. She held out her foot. Her toe throbbed with pain. "A sliver," he informed her with a shake of his head. "Tending to students' medical needs is not my usual duty." He took a small device from his waistcoat pocket. Even though they didn't use such devices in her kingdom, she knew all about phones. He tapped the screen. "I have summoned a nurse fairy." Then he frowned in disapproval. "Why are you not wearing the correct apparel for your feet?"

Meeshell gulped. There'd been no time to get shoes before she left. The decision to send her to school had happened so quickly. Her mother had placed clothing orders, but they hadn't arrived before her departure, so the packages were supposed to be delivered to her at school. She held her foot. "I..." How was she to know that feet were so delicate? She'd never worn them before.

In a burst of blue light, a tiny winged creature appeared before her. It zipped around her head, then perched on her foot. Oh barnacles, did that ever tickle! Meeshell gritted her teeth and held as still as possible. The fairy peered over her big toe. Then it touched a wand to the sliver and, voilà, the pain was gone. In another burst of light, the fairy disappeared before Meeshell had the chance to say thank you.

"Better?" the headmaster asked.

Meeshell nodded. The pain was gone and there wasn't even a red mark where the sliver had been.

"Our nurse fairies do a very good job," he told her. "Let us hope you won't have to call upon them again." Then he resumed their walk.

She followed the headmaster across the beach and up a sandy trail. He walked with long strides, and didn't stumble or wobble the way she did. "Do

you think there's something wrong with my legs?" Meeshell asked.

He peered down his long nose at her. "I beg your pardon but I'm having trouble hearing you." The gulls were no longer screeching, and the waves lapped gently in the distance, so there wasn't much to compete with Meeshell's voice.

"I'm sorry." She put her hand to her throat. "I can't seem to speak very loudly. It's...odd."

He raised an eyebrow. "Indeed."

She cleared her throat and tried again. "Do you think there's something wrong with my legs?"

"How so?"

"They feel so unsteady. Maybe I didn't get the right kind."

"I'm sure the Sea Witch gave you perfectly adequate legs. She has no reason to do otherwise. She wants you to be successful here."

The headmaster possessed a commanding voice that was reassuring in its confidence, but also a bit frightening in its authority. This was the man who'd

summoned Meeshell to Ever After High. He'd sent a letter to her parents insisting that she attend. And he'd convinced the Sea Witch to help by giving her a pair of legs.

She looked down at those legs, hidden beneath the long, yellow dress. There was no reason to suspect they were faulty or badly formed. It was, as the headmaster pointed out, in the Sea Witch's best interest that Meeshell and her new legs succeed at Ever After High.

For Meeshell had something the Sea Witch wanted.

Chapter 3

Watery Witch

The events that led up to Meeshell's journey happened as quickly as a riptide. First, Headmaster Grimm's message arrived in a bottle, carried by United Manta Ray. Her parents read the message, then they summoned her. "Meeshell," her mother said. "We have news. You are going on a trip tomorrow morning."

"Tomorrow morning?" Meeshell asked, both surprised and confused. "But I've got school."

The family had gathered in the castle's main room. Meeshell's mother and father were the queen and king

19

of the Merpeople, which made Meeshell a princess.
But their palace was not a sprawling fortress. Unlike
land-dwellers, the Merpeople did not build immense
structures. Rather, they lived in harmony with their
surroundings, down deep where fishermen's nets and
lines did not go. This castle was an elegant cave,
lighted by magical jewels that were embedded in the
walls. Hermit crabs made little trails in the sandy
floor, and butterfly fish swam gracefully near the
entrance. Storms did not rage that deep, and sharks
did not prowl. It was a lovely, peaceful place, with no
dangers to speak of.

Well, except for the Sea Witch.

But she lived in her own cave, on the other side
of the kelp forest. And she'd made a pact with the
king and queen. She would not bother them as long
as they stuck to the story and gave her their firstborn daughter's voice. Meeshell's voice.

Meeshell's mother was the famous Little Mermaid. As a young woman, she'd agreed to give her
beautiful voice to the Sea Witch in exchange for

legs and the chance to live on land. And so the deal was made, and the Little Mermaid went to live among the land-dwellers, leaving behind the most beautiful singing voice in all the Merworld. But as is true in many fairytales, there is often a way to elude a witch's dark magic: true love. In the Little Mermaid's case, when she found the true love of a prince and he agreed to live beneath the sea with her, the curse was broken. Her voice returned to her.

Which left the Sea Witch without a beautiful mermaid voice to complete her collection. This sent the witch into such a rage that the sea roiled and frothed like a witch's cauldron.

So now the Sea Witch had to wait for the day when the Little Mermaid's firstborn daughter would live the story her mother was supposed to have lived—to permanently exchange her voice for legs and life on land.

And wait the Sea Witch did, counting the days until she got Meeshell's voice.

"You will not be going to Merschool tomorrow

because you will be going to a different school," her mother explained.

"Why?"

"You have been invited to attend Ever After High," her father said, a proud smile on his handsome face.

Meeshell pondered this news. Ever After High? Her father often spoke of the school he'd attended. He'd loved it. She remembered many bedtime stories about his days fighting dragons in Dragon-Slaying class and climbing towers in Hero Training class. How he'd been co-president of the student body, and captain of the Track and Shield team. The world above the waves was so very different. For Meeshell and her Merfriends, school studies focused on learning about the other creatures that inhabited the sea. There were no class presidents or clubs or teams. Her people considered themselves the guardians of the waters, and thus, taking care of other creatures was of the utmost importance.

"But Ever After High is *on land*, and I'm not supposed to go onto land until I'm older," Meeshell said. "My story isn't supposed to start yet. Is it?"

Her mother swam over and handed Meeshell the message-in-a-bottle. It had been written on water-proof paper.

From the desk of
HEADMASTER GRIMM

Dear Philip and Pearl,

I believe it is in your daughter's best interest to begin her studies, posthaste, at Ever After High. While Merschool is suitable for those who will live out their lives in the sea, I believe it is not the best choice for a young princess whose destiny is to eventually live on land. Ever After High will provide Meeshell the everyday experiences that will prepare her for her future life as a land-dweller. Fall quarter begins in three days. A dormitory room shall be waiting for her.

> Yours ever after,
> Headmaster Grimm

PS—I have sent an urgent message to the Sea Witch, asking her to help with Meeshell's transformation.

"The Sea Witch?" An icy feeling darted up Meeshell's spine. The scales on her tail shivered.

"Unfortunately, she is the only one who possesses the magic to give you legs," her mother explained.

"I know but..." This was all so very confusing. When Meeshell woke up that morning, she'd been looking forward to learning stingray songs. But now her life was being turned upside down. "But..."

"Sweetheart, I know you must feel like you've been hit by a tidal wave," her mother said gently. She took Meeshell's hand. "But this isn't bad news. It's good news. This is a wonderful opportunity. When I went onto land, I barely knew anything. I'd only observed people from a distance, so it was very difficult for me. But you'll get the chance to live with people, to learn directly from them. And when you make that final transition to living permanently on land, it won't be so shocking."

That all made sense, but it didn't change the fact that Meeshell wasn't ready to leave. "But that means

I have to go away." She tried to bravely hold back her tears.

"Only for a while. You'll have long weekends and holiday breaks to come home. And there's summer, of course." Her dad took her other hand. "You'll have so much fun, the time will fly by."

But how could she have fun without her friends? And then another thought struck her.

"What about Finbert?" Meeshell asked. She reached out her hand. A tiny narwhal swam over. She stroked his back. Finbert had been her beloved pet since she was a baby. She couldn't stand the thought of them being apart for such long periods of time.

"Finbert can join you after you've settled in," her father replied with a smile. "You will see that several of your classmates at Ever After High have pets."

Well, at least that was something. "Did you hear that, Finbert?" she asked. "You can join me later." He nodded, then chased after a puffer fish.

Suddenly, the water turned cold. A sharp current shot through the castle, swirling around Meeshell and her parents. The hermit crabs tucked into their shells. The butterfly fish darted into a crevice. Something was coming.

The Sea Witch entered. Her tail differed from most of her fellow Merpeople. Not made of glistening scales, it was built of red armor, like a crab's shell.

At the sight of the witch, Queen Pearl pulled her daughter close. King Philip grabbed his trident and rose into a protective stance. The Sea Witch stopped swimming and waved a hand at him. "Oh, calm down, Philip. I'm not here to stir up the waters. I got a message from Milton Grimm, same as you."

The king lowered his trident. "You'll help us?" he asked warily.

"Help *you*?" She cackled as all witches do, whether on land or in water. "I'm not here to help *you*! You two and your true love kept me from adding a beautiful mermaid voice to my collection."

"If you're not going to help us, then why are you here?" Queen Pearl asked.

"I'm here to help myself, of course!" Her voice was as rough and scratchy as sand. Her long, tangled black hair floated around her head. A few crabs peeked out from among the tangles. She pointed a finger at Meeshell. "If I give you legs, and you go to school, and you make lots of friends, and you meet a dashing prince, blah blah blah, then you will fall in love with living on land and you will embrace your destiny. And I will have your voice!" More cackling.

"You can't have her voice until she decides to stay on land permanently," Queen Pearl pointed out. "And that won't happen until after she's graduated."

"Yeah, yeah, details, details. Whatever." The Sea Witch rolled her black eyes. "I only care about one thing: completing my collection!" Then she hollered, "Coral! Where are you?"

Another mermaid swam into the palace. Coral, daughter of the Sea Witch, was a few years younger

than Meeshell. She had dark, blue-black hair and a red tail like her mother.

"Seeing as this is a special request, I'm going to let my daughter cast the spell. She could use the practice."

Coral smiled nervously. "Yeah, my last spell didn't go so well." Meeshell's parents shared a troubled glance. Coral's botched spells were well-known in the Merworld.

The Sea Witch chuckled. "Never mind that, darling. That stupid shark seems fine with his new head of hair. We all make mistakes. That's part of learning." The Sea Witch patted her daughter's head.

"Do you think this is a good idea?" King Philip asked the witch. "Shouldn't you be the one to cast the spell?"

"Of course it's a good idea!" the Sea Witch bellowed. "Coral is perfectly capable of replacing a Mertail with two human legs. Right, Coral?"

It took Coral a few moments before she nodded, and even then, she didn't look confident. Meeshell

gulped. Her hand flew to her tail, to its soft, blue scales.

The Sea Witch spun around, then swam toward the entry. "Meet us at dawn, on the shore of Turtle Island." And with another blast of cold current, she was gone. After a little wave good-bye, Coral followed.

"Is this really happening?" Meeshell asked her parents.

"Yes," they both said. Which was not the answer she'd hoped for.

Flotation

Device

$\mathscr{S}$and and pebbles crunched beneath Meeshell's bare feet as she followed the headmaster up the path. "Are you still resolute about hiding your true identity?" he asked.

"Yes." She'd thought about this during her sea voyage. And she'd discussed it at length with her parents before leaving the Merworld. If her future was to live on land, and to be two-footed, then it was important for her to gain acceptance among the

students as an equal. To not be treated differently. If the students and teachers knew she'd spent most of her life with a tail, they might not expect as much from her. She didn't want that. She wanted the true experience. If everyone thought she was a human, they'd treat her as a human.

The trail rounded a corner and the beach disappeared from view. The headmaster folded his arms behind his back as they walked. He didn't try to force conversation. She couldn't tell if he agreed or disagreed with her decision to hide her true identity. They continued in silence, up the path and onto a cobbled road.

She'd just been getting used to the sandy terrain, but cobblestones were a totally different sensation. Her ankles twisted as she stepped into the ruts between the stones. How did people do this? Swimming came naturally to Merpeople—they didn't need to be taught. But walking was so weird! "How long does it take someone to learn to walk?" she asked.

The headmaster turned, glancing at her from beneath his bushy brows. "Some start walking after nine months, but for others it can take more than a year." More than a year? What had she gotten herself into?

They traversed a pretty wooden drawbridge, then stood at the entrance to the campus. An elegant archway loomed overhead, its face carved with the words: *Welcome to Ever After High.*

Meeshell's skin got all tingly. It was as if she'd just discovered a new world. Certainly she'd seen parts of this world up close. She'd encountered many boats, both those run by fishermen, and huge cruise ships overflowing with land-dwellers. And she'd watched humans walking along the beach, swimming, sunning themselves. But to stand in their world…it felt like a dream.

The school was so much larger than she'd imagined. The stone buildings looked big enough to fit giants. Wide walkways wound between colorful gardens where everything was in bloom. The flowers were all unfamiliar to Meeshell, but they were beautiful. A unicorn fountain stood at the center of a pool, where white swans nibbled on water bugs between lily pads. But what struck her most was that there were mirrors everywhere she looked. On the trees, on the walls; one even hung from a tiny white cloud.

The campus was oddly quiet. She'd expected lots of people and activity. Her father had always described it that way. She looked around.

"The students are gathered in the Charmitorium for a School Spirit assembly," the headmaster explained. "The cheerhexers are leading the assembly, to show support for our athletic teams." Right on cue, a loud cheer rose from a nearby building. A dreamy, faraway look filled the headmaster's eyes. "Back in my day, I played center on the basketball team. I held the record for most baskets of food dunked in a single game. Those wolves could never catch me. Ah, I remember those days as if they were yesterday."

Meeshell tried to imagine a game like that, but her attention was diverted by a large brown rabbit sitting on a bench. Meeshell had seen rabbits before, hopping about on shore, but this one wore glasses. And was reading a book! And were those horns sprouting from his head? Then she squealed as something bumped into her foot. She stepped aside as three roundish creatures, covered in prickles like sea urchins, waddled past. They made funny snorting noises at her. She shielded her eyes with her hand and looked up at the sky as a large shape passed overhead. "Was that a dragon?" she asked.

"Indeed."

Her father had told many stories about dragons. They terrified villagers and stole treasure. They reminded her of sharks.

"You have no reason to be concerned," the headmaster explained. "All the Ever After High dragons are friendly. We don't allow dangerous dragons here. There's a protective spell to keep them away."

That was a relief. It was bad enough encountering

a shark, but having to worry about something swooping down from the sky seemed unbearable. Meeshell followed the headmaster up a wide stone stairway. As the headmaster approached, a pair of doors flew open. He and Meeshell stepped into the Administration Building.

A tree grew in the center of the building, its branches reaching into the corners and its trunk disappearing right through the ceiling. Birds nestled in the branches. A pink squirrel scurried around the trunk. There was a mirror on this tree, too.

Up a staircase Meeshell and the headmaster went, spiraling 'round and 'round until they reached the upper floor. They passed through another door and into a room, where a lady sat at a desk. She had extremely large ears and an oversized nose from which long, black hairs sprouted. The sign on her desk read:

> ## NO STUDENT SEEN WITHOUT AN APPOINTMENT

The headmaster spoke to her. "Mrs. Trollworth, this is our newest student, Meeshell. Do you have her student file?"

"Does she have an appointment? She can't be here without an appointment." She tapped the sign with a stubby finger.

"There's no need for an appointment. I just met her at the dock and now we need to find her new student file."

"Yeah, okay, it's here somewhere." The troll lady shuffled through a very large stack of papers, tossing some over her shoulder onto another large stack. It was quite messy behind her desk. She found what looked like an old sandwich, took a bite, then tossed it aside. After riffling through another stack of papers she exclaimed, "Got it!" She handed over the file. Then she stared at Meeshell's bare feet, which had picked up quite a bit of dirt during the walk. "You part troll?" she asked. Meeshell didn't understand the question, until she noticed that the troll lady's feet were also bare. Except hers were hairy, with gnarly yellow toenails.

Meeshell shook her head.

"Oh. Too bad for you." She plopped onto her chair and began to eat noisily from a bag of salted cockroach crisps.

"Right this way." Headmaster Grimm escorted Meeshell into his office. A massive carved desk sat in the center of the room. The walls were covered with framed photos of various members of the Grimm family. But what really caught Meeshell's attention was the elderly woman who was sitting on a cushion and floating about four feet off the ground. She looked very comfortable. Meeshell suddenly missed the sensation of floating—missed the way the water held and cradled her.

"Hello," the woman said. Her voice was craggy with age, but kind. Snarled gray hair peeked out from a scarf she wore over her head. A pair of golden bangles hung from her earlobes.

"Meeshell, this is Professor Baba Yaga. She is the department head for Spells, Hexes, and General Witchery classes. Because you are not a witch, you will not likely find yourself in one of her classrooms. However, she volunteered to keep an eye on you during your stay here."

"I have a keen interest in you. I was your father's advisor when he attended this school. I remember him well." She floated closer. "You have his eyes."

Meeshell gulped. This professor knew her identity? She looked questioningly at the headmaster.

"You can't hide the truth from Professor Yaga," he said. "And she feels it is very important to monitor your health."

"My health?"

"Yes," Professor Yaga said. "Please, sit." She motioned toward a chair. Meeshell sat. She went to tuck her tail beneath the chair, but then remembered the new legs. She crossed them at the ankles, imagining that they'd once again become a tail.

The headmaster walked behind his desk and sat in a chair so large, it looked like a throne. Professor Yaga pressed her fingertips together and floated a bit higher, looking down at Meeshell. "Your health is of my utmost concern. Leaving the water is not a simple feat. Your body is not used to gravity."

"Oh." Meeshell thought about this for a moment. "Is that why I feel heavier?"

"Exactly. You are used to the buoyancy of water. I noticed that when you walked in, you were a bit wobbly on your legs. I wouldn't worry about that. You're young and strong; you should adapt quickly."

"Coral, the Sea Witch's daughter, cast the spell, and she said that when she tried it on an eel, the eel's new legs fell off. Do you think that might happen to me?"

"Let us hope not!" Professor Yaga gave Meeshell a very lengthy stare. "I'm wondering about your voice. Is that as loud as you can speak?"

"Yes, I'm having trouble. My voice feels…weak."

"Ah, another effect of being out of water. Your vocal cords are used to both air and water, but not to air one hundred percent of the time. It's having a negative effect on them."

"Could the air *damage* my voice?" Meeshell asked, her brow furrowed.

Professor Yaga narrowed her eyes. "It is a possibility." Then she gave the headmaster an odd look. Meeshell uncrossed her legs and sat up straight. Was it possible her voice wouldn't be fine? This could be a very big deal because her story centered on her voice!

"I can see that you're concerned." Professor Yaga floated closer again, then patted Meeshell's shoulder. "Let's not panic. Perhaps all your voice needs is time to adjust. I will keep a close eye on you and check in with you often. But if anything changes, let me know right away." And off she floated.

Once again, Meeshell's hand flew to her throat. If this trip to Ever After High ruined her voice, the Sea Witch would be furious! And without a voice to trade, Meeshell's story line would be ruined.

"I have the highest confidence in Professor Yaga," Headmaster Grimm told her. "You are in extremely capable hands. When Faybelle Thorn cast an evil spell and it backfired, taking away Faybelle's ability to fly, Professor Yaga guided her through the recovery process. And recover she did. That young fairy ignores the campus flying speed limit every chance she gets." He cleared his throat, then opened Meeshell's file. "Now, there is some business we must attend to. Because you wish to keep your identity a secret while you're here, we think it would be best to give you a single room."

Meeshell agreed that things might be easier if she had total privacy, but it felt like special treatment. "Do other students have single rooms?"

"No."

"If I get my own room, won't that make other students suspicious?" Her throat felt tickly as she spoke. "I want to be treated like everyone else."

"Very well." He leaned forward and hollered, "Mrs. Trollworth!"

The troll lady poked her large head into his office. "What?"

"Meeshell needs a roommate assignment."

The troll lady disappeared, followed by more sounds of papers being flung about, then she stuck her head back in. "There's an empty bed in room twelve-C."

"Twelve-C?" he asked.

"Yeah. Farrah Goodfairy."

"I see." He stroked his chin for a moment. "Farrah Goodfairy is not royalty. Will that matter to you?"

Meeshell shrugged. "Should it?"

At her school in the Merkingdom, most of Meeshell's classmates were not princes or princesses. In fact, none of her closest friends from her old school were royalty. Things like that simply didn't matter to her.

"It has long been a tradition, here at Ever After High, to house royals together. It makes sense, based on their shared school curriculums and traditions. But lately we've been embracing diversification. I

think Farrah might be a good match for you. She's very intelligent and exceptionally friendly." He wrote something into Meeshell's file. "Very well. Twelve-C it is. Now that we have that matter settled, a member of the Welcoming Committee should be here shortly to show you around."

And at that very moment, a girl stepped into the office. She smiled so brightly at Meeshell that, for a moment, all of Meeshell's worries faded away.

An Apple

a Day

*H*eadmaster Grimm stood and a wide grin spread across his face. Whoever this girl was, she was very well liked. "Well, this is a lovely surprise. What can I do for you?" he asked.

"She doesn't have an appointment!" the troll lady hollered from the other room.

The girl called out to the ornery receptionist, "It's okay, Mrs. Trollworth. I didn't make an appointment because I'm not here to see the headmaster."

She turned and smiled again at Meeshell. "Briar Beauty usually greets new students, since she's head of the Ever After High Welcoming Committee, but she couldn't leave the Spirit assembly, so she sent me. I've applied to be a member of the committee. You're my first official new student." The girl's cheeks were round and dimpled, and her blue eyes twinkled. They *actually* twinkled. She held out her hand. "I'm Apple. Apple White."

"Hi." Meeshell shyly reached out and shook her hand. "I'm…Meeshell."

"No last name?" Apple asked. Meeshell shook her head. "Oh, how enchanting! One name, just like Cinderella. Well, Meeshell, I'm fairy, fairy happy to meet you."

"Are you…?" Meeshell's voice was barely a whisper. She knew that she'd be meeting all sorts of well-known students, but this girl was related to the most famous woman in the entire fairytale world! "Are you *Snow White's* daughter?"

"Yes, but don't let that sway your opinion of me. Seriously, my mom is wonderful, but in most ways she's just like everyone else's mom. She checks in on me all the time, wanting to know if I'm getting enough sleep, if I'm flossing, and if I'm eating healthy. And she always wants to know if I have a *boyfriend*." She giggled. "I'm much too busy studying to worry about that sort of thing." She reached into a book bag and pulled out a red apple. "This is a little welcome gift for you. Don't worry, it's not a *poisoned apple*." Apple giggled again. "I don't poison apples; I just eat poisoned apples. At least, I'm supposed to, one day."

Meeshell took the apple. It certainly was beautiful. She'd eaten apples, but only the golden kind. There was a place near her home where an ancient apple tree grew close to shore, its branches hanging out over the water. She and her friends would wait for the fruit to fall, then sit on the beach and eat their fill. But she'd never tasted a red apple.

"Go on, give it a try. It's a hybrid, grown special in my kingdom. Mom ships crates of them to me."

Meeshell took a bite. She was surprised by the combination of tart and sweet. "Yum," she said. She wiped a bit of juice that dribbled down her chin.

"I know, isn't it the best?" Apple took another one out of her bag and set it onto the headmaster's desk. "Headmaster Grimm, what is Meeshell's dorm assignment?" she asked.

"She shall be rooming with Ms. Goodfairy," he said.

Apple clapped her hands. "Oh, you'll love Farrah! She's a spelltacular girl, and a hexcellent student! Come on, let's go. I have so much to show you. Good-bye, Headmaster Grimm. Charm you later!"

The headmaster grabbed Meeshell's bag and handed it to her. "Good-bye, Ms. White and Ms.… ahem…Meeshell. Remember, Professor Yaga will act as your advisor, should you need anything."

"Thank you."

Apple placed another apple onto Mrs. Trolworth's desk. "I don't like apples!" the troll lady bellowed, reaching for a handful of cockroach crisps.

"Oh, Mrs. Trollworth, haven't you heard the saying—an apple a day keeps the doctor away?" Apple asked sweetly.

"What's that supposed to mean?" Mrs. Trollworth asked grumpily.

"It means apples are good for you."

As they left, Mrs. Trollworth called, "Hey, this one doesn't have any worms in it. Next time you bring me an apple, I want one with worms!"

When Apple led Meeshell down the stairs, her red skirt flounced with her excited footsteps. "I like your yellow dress. It's very…old-fashioned," she said diplomatically. "But what happened to your shoes?"

"Um, well, I came by boat and…" Meeshell wasn't sure what to say.

"Oh dear." Apple gasped. "Did a giant squid take them? That happened to my aunt once. She took a cruise to the North Pole and a giant squid ate the whole boat. Luckily, he spat out my aunt, but he kept her shoes. Isn't that mean?" Meeshell didn't respond. She'd met a few giant squids and they were the opposite of mean. In fact, they were the shyest creatures in the ocean. But she knew that legends often portrayed them as dangerous beasts. The very last thing giant squids wanted to do was to attack anyone or anything. They preferred napping and weaving. And they certainly didn't eat boats or shoes. "I'll help you get a new pair. We have the best shoe store in the village."

"Thanks," Meeshell said.

"So, how come you're whispering?"

"There's something wrong with my voice." Meeshell felt her cheeks burn. Apple must think she was so strange, with her whispery voice.

But Apple just gave her a sympathetic smile. "I'm royally sorry to hear that. If it gets worse I can pick up some throat lozenges at the infirmary. The pickled pepper lozenges taste terrible, but they work great."

The doors to the Administration Building flew open and the girls stepped outside. The campus was still quiet. "Since this is my first official Welcome Committee assignment, I need to check my list," Apple explained. She pulled a little piece of paper from her pocket. "Let's see, first I meet you, then I'm supposed to take you to the bookstore to get supplies. It's right over there."

As they walked across the quad, Apple chatted happily. "I remember my first day at school. I was super hexcited because I'd requested Raven Queen for my roommate and I got her. I spent most of the morning decorating our room. She didn't like it, not at first. And I think she was shocked that the girl she's supposed to poison was her roommate and wanted to be her friend. It took her a while to get used to me but now we're BFFAs. That's best friends forever after." She smiled at Meeshell. "You'll make friends right away. In fact, that's one of the things

on my list. Look." She pointed to the list and read. "'*Help the New Student Make Friends*.' Everyone here is really nice. Well, not *everyone*. There are some villains, but a fairytale wouldn't be a fairytale without villains." She stopped in her tracks and raised her eyebrow. "Are you a villain?"

Meeshell shook her head.

"I didn't think so. I'm a fairy good judge of people and you don't strike me as a villain. What is your story? Oh, wait, never mind that right now because here's the bookstore."

Hoping to avoid more conversation about her "story," Meeshell darted into the bookstore. It was a crowded place, with floor-to-ceiling shelves. Besides books, there were all sorts of things to buy, each adorned with the Ever After High emblem—water bottles, socks, and hoodies to name a few. There was an entire section dedicated to Daring Charming. Meeshell had read a lot about Prince Charming, but she wasn't familiar with his son. Daring's handsome face adorned T-shirts, book bags, and key chains.

"Daring's got a whole fan club," Apple explained. "We dated for a while but, right now, I'm way too busy for romance. What about you? Do you have a boyfriend back home?"

Meeshell shook her head. She had friends, lots of friends, but never a real boyfriend. There'd been that one time, when Splash, a boy she went to school with, had held her hand. And had kissed her cheek in the moonlight. But she didn't feel anything deeper than friendship for him.

Apple picked up a Daring Charming water bottle. "I figure there will always be boys to date. But we only get to go to this school for a short time, and I want to make the most of my education while I'm here." She set the bottle aside, then walked up to the counter. The cashier had green hair and pointed ears. "Hi, Birch. This is Meeshell, a new student. She needs to pick up a MirrorPad."

"Welcome to Ever After High," he said. Then he handed Meeshell a black square thing.

"What is this?" Meeshell asked.

"You don't know?" Though Apple sounded surprised, she didn't seem to judge Meeshell, which was a huge relief. "Well, here at Ever After High, we have a Mirror Network. That's the fastest way to communicate. With this MirrorPad, you can watch the latest MirrorCasts, communicate with other students, get your class thronework assignments, send hexts to your family, basically everything. Yesterday my mom sent a photo of our family cat. Isn't she cute?" She pulled out her own MirrorPad, touched the screen, and a snow-white cat appeared, wearing a cute jeweled red collar. Meeshell suddenly missed Finbert. "Oh look, I have a MirrorMail from Ashlynn. She wants to meet up for lunch."

"Wow," Meeshell said, amazed by the technology. The Merkingdom didn't have anything like this. If she wanted to meet up with her Merfriends, she used the conch shell to call them, and then they'd meet at their favorite kelp grotto.

"Thanks, Birch," Apple said.

"No problem."

Outside the bookstore, Apple and Meeshell sat on a wooden bench. "Okay, now that we have your MirrorPad, let's look at your class schedule." Apple opened Meeshell's MirrorPad, touched the screen a few times, and a schedule appeared.

> Student: First Name: Meeshell.
> Last Name: Withheld.

Apple pursed her lips and glanced at Meeshell. "Why does it say 'withheld'?"

"Uh, some kind of mistake?" Meeshell suggested.

"Well, you definitely have a full schedule and, oh look, you're in Princessology. I didn't know you were a royal. But where's your crown?" Apple touched her own crown.

Meeshell didn't normally wear a crown. Instead, she preferred a pearl headband, which she'd tucked into her small bag, along with a few of her very special belongings.

Apple looked concerned. "Oh dear. Did that

giant squid take your crown, too? We'll be sure to get you a new one. We can probably order it and have it delivered. What kingdom are you from?"

Even though she'd had those three days on the ship to ponder all the potential questions, Meeshell hadn't quite worked out all the details of her alias. She'd been distracted by her new legs, and the great effort it took getting used to them. "I'm from very far away. Across the ocean. You've never heard of it, I'm sure."

"I took Geografairy last year and aced it. We had to study *all* the kingdoms. Let me guess." Apple scrunched up her face as she thought deeply. "Since you came across the ocean, is it…is it the Kingdom by the Sea?"

Meeshell nodded. She felt bad about starting her friendship with a lie but if she told Apple where she came from, then Apple would immediately know she was a mermaid. As warm of a welcome she was getting from Apple, Meeshell still believed that, in the long run, it would be best if everyone at

Ever After High thought she was just a normal, two-footed princess.

Apple placed a hand on Meeshell's shoulder. "This is probably your first time being away from home. We all get homesick at first. But it will pass, I promise. You'll start to feel as if this is your second home in no time. And one of the best ways to fight homesickness is to make new friends." Meeshell was speechless. This very nice student, whom she'd just met, was being so kind. Would everyone be like this? Apple glanced at her list. "It says here that I'm supposed to get you signed up for at least one club or sports team. What are your interests?"

Meeshell wasn't sure what to say. Back home, she really loved riding manta rays. In fact, she was a champion, having won first place in her age group in the manta ray race. She also loved combing the seafloor for treasures. While the Sea Witch collected voices, Meeshell collected shells of all shapes and sizes. And she was really good at sea languages, having mastered Porpoise *and* Dolphin. But none of

those interests seemed right for Ever After High. "Well, I'm not really sure what my interests are," she said. Then she coughed. Her throat felt so scratchy.

"*Oooh*, we need to get you those lozenges."

Sounds arose in the distance. The doors to the Charmitorium flew open and students began to emerge. "Oh look, the assembly is over. It's time for lunch. Come on, let's get you something to eat and you can meet some of the other students. And then I can cross one more thing off the list: help the new student make friends."

pple was taking her Welcoming Committee role very seriously: Each time she and Meeshell passed something she'd say, "Welcome to the drinking fountain." "Welcome to the wishing well." "Welcome to the exterior hallway of the Student Union Building." She certainly seemed very nice, and her desire to make Meeshell feel at home at Ever After High seemed genuine. Her warm smile put Meeshell at ease. But it was a bit unnerving for Meeshell to think that one day Apple would be

poisoned by an apple and lie in a coma, waiting for true love's kiss. The truth was, many of Ever After High's students, including Meeshell, had stories that would require sacrifice and courage.

"Welcome to the Castleteria!" Apple exclaimed, throwing her arms wide.

The Castleteria bustled with activity as hungry students hurried in from the assembly, eager to grab lunch. There was so much commotion, and so many people, Meeshell wished she were a hermit crab and could disappear into a shell. Some of the students cast curious glances at Meeshell's old dress. One student, a human-sized fairy with blond hair and iridescent wings, flew up to her and said with a sneer, "I didn't realize that today was Wear Your Grand-mother's Old Dress Day." Then she flew off. Meeshell felt her cheeks go red for the second time that day.

"Don't mind her," Apple said. "Her name is Faybelle and she *never* says anything nice. Besides, wearing old clothing is called being retro and it's very in style right now."

Lots of students said hello to Apple, who in turn introduced Meeshell, but the names and faces came so quickly, Meeshell was certain she wouldn't remember a single one. Her gaze darted around the dining hall. Large trees grew along the walls, their branches reaching high above tables that were arranged in tidy rows. The kitchen area was its own vast room. Another tree grew in the center, copper pans hanging from its branches. Cauldrons bubbled on dragon-fire hearths and baskets overflowed with colorful vegetables and fruits. Students grabbed trays and lined up at a long counter to choose from a wide array of foods. Apple handed Meeshell a tray. Meeshell tried to forget the mean fairy's comment but as she looked around, it was quite obvious that her dress *wasn't* in fashion.

A hunchbacked woman stood behind the counter. She held a ladle that overflowed with something gray and gooey. A box labeled LUMPS sat at her elbow. Apple whispered in Meeshell's ear, "That's

porridge. Hagatha serves it all day long. Blondie Lockes likes it a lot but I suggest you avoid it. It's the worst." When they reached the woman, Apple introduced them. "Hagatha, this is our new student, Meeshell. Meeshell, Hagatha is our Castleteria cook."

"Got any food allergies?" Hagatha asked, wiping her hand on her greasy apron. Meeshell shook her head. "Got any special dietary needs?"

Meeshell hadn't noticed any sea-lettuce salads or barnacle stew in the food choices, but she didn't want to make special requests. She needed to eat the same things the other two-footed people ate. But there was one thing she couldn't stomach. "I don't eat fish."

Hagatha grunted. "I don't blame ya. Fish are slimy things. I don't eat them neither." *Slimy* wasn't a word Meeshell would use to describe the ocean's most beautiful creatures. Her eyes widened as- Hagatha dumped a ladle of porridge into a bowl, then

set the bowl onto Meeshell's tray. The porridge jiggled a bit, as if it were going to jump out of the bowl, but then it settled into a mound.

"This will make it taste better," Apple said as she grabbed a honey bear. The bear giggled as she picked it up and squeezed.

Because Meeshell was obviously overwhelmed and a bit confused, Apple helpfully selected a few more items for Meeshell's tray—a cucumber sandwich, a miniature thronecake, and a glass of fairyberry iced tea. Then she led her to a table. "Everyone, I want you to meet our newest student, Meeshell. She's a princess from the Kingdom by the Sea."

One by one she was introduced. "This is Ashlynn Ella, daughter of Cinderella. She works at the Glass Slipper, which is the best shoe store in all the kingdoms. And she speaks to animals, which comes in handy if you get stuck in a tower and you need a griffin to come and rescue you."

"Yes, Griffinglish is my favorite animal language,"

Ashlynn said. A delicate crown was nestled on her long, strawberry-blonde hair, which flowed over her shoulders.

The next girl had wavy, milk-chocolate-colored hair and a pair of crownglasses perched on her head. "This is Briar Beauty, daughter of Sleeping Beauty. She's the best party planner on campus, and even though she tends to fall asleep *a lot*, don't let that fool you. She's always up for a fun adventure."

Briar waved. "Welcome to—" Her words were interrupted by a huge yawn.

A shiver ran up Meeshell's spine. She was meeting the daughters of the best-known fairytale characters ever after! This was amazing.

"And this is Madeline Hatter, daughter of the Mad Hatter. We call her Maddie."

Meeshell paused. She didn't recognize the Hatter name. Must be from a story she'd never read. The girl was very colorful, with stripes and polka dots and swirls on her clothing. Her hair was equally

colorful, with stripes of turquoise, purple, and blue. An odd little teacup hat sat on her head.

Maddie grabbed Meeshell's hand and shook it quite vigorously. "Hello and good-bye. I like to say both those things because it saves time. When we save time in Wonderland, we put it into a jar so we can use it later." Her personality was as exuberant as her outfit. Meeshell liked her right away.

"It's nice to meet you," Meeshell said. There was so much noise in the Castleteria from all the chatter, she could barely hear her own voice.

"Uh, what was that?" Maddie asked.

Briar cleaned her crownglasses with a napkin. "I think she said it's nice to eat stew."

Maddie nodded. "Well, who can argue with that?"

Apple squeezed in next to Maddie. Ashlynn scooted down the bench to make room for Meeshell, who placed her tray on the table and sat.

Ashlynn glanced down and gasped. "Your feet," she said.

Meeshell bit her lower lip. Was it obvious that

her feet were brand-new? Or was something actually wrong with them, as she'd suspected.

But Ashlynn was smiling. "They're the prettiest feet I've ever seen. No wonder you don't wear any shoes."

"She lost her shoes on her journey here," Apple explained. "They were stolen by a giant squid."

"Awesome," Briar said. "I've always wanted to see one of those."

Apple stirred sugar into her tea. "I thought you could take her to the Glass Slipper and help her choose some new ones."

"I've got a better idea," Ashlynn said. "We'll use the new app and order a pair right now. What size do you wear?"

Size? Meeshell gulped. How could she possible know a thing like that? She must have looked very confused because Ashlynn smiled kindly.

"Oh, I get it. You probably always have your shoes ordered for you, so why would you know the size?"

"Uh, yes, that's it," Meeshell said.

Ashlynn placed her MirrorPad under Meeshell's feet to measure their size, then selected a few pairs to be delivered to her room. "Easy as pie."

"Hey, wanna see my tea-rrific new talent show trick?" Maddie took off her hat and began to pull out a stack of teacups. The stack got taller and taller. How could all those cups fit inside that tiny hat?

"It's a magic hat," Apple explained. "She keeps *everything* in there."

Maddie held the wobbling stack of teacups, which now reached to the ceiling. "Look," she said proudly. "It's the Leaning Tower of Tea-sa!" Right when she said that, the tower collapsed, spilling tea all over the table. A giant puddle formed and began to move toward Meeshell. She dropped her porridge spoon, her eyes widening. If the puddle rolled off the edge, it would land in her lap. It would land on *her legs*! She shrieked, jumped to her feet, and stepped away.

Maddie frowned. "Well, that didn't go as planned, but you know what they say in Wonderland—there's no use crying over spilled tea when you can sing over it instead." As she started to hum a little song, a pair of cleaning fairies flew over and began mopping up the mess.

"You okay?" Apple asked Meeshell. "You look startled."

Meeshell checked her legs. They were perfectly dry. She let out a long, relieved breath. "I'm fine."

"You didn't get tea stains on your dress, did you?" Ashlynn asked.

"My favorite color is tea stain," Maddie said. "It's pretty *and* it's delicious at the same time."

"No, there aren't any stains," Meeshell replied. The fairies cleaned the bench, then flew away with their little mops.

"You sure you're okay?" Briar asked. The girls were all looking at her, probably wondering about her strange behavior. Who shrieks when tea is spilled? Was Meeshell already getting a reputation as an oddball?

"Are you afraid of tea?" Maddie asked.

"No, I'm…I'm not afraid of tea." Meeshell's heart beat quickly. That had been a very close call. Too close for comfort. And because she was quite flustered, she said the first thing that she could think of. "I'm…I'm afraid of water."

It was absurd, of course, to think that a mermaid could be afraid of water. But, for the first time in Meeshell's life, there was some truth to this statement, because the spell that had given Meeshell the ability to walk on two legs had a flaw.

And it was all because of Coral, the Sea Witch's daughter.

Coral's

Spell

Three Days Ago

They met at dawn on the shore of Turtle Island. The turtles were a bit annoyed by the interruption. They narrowed their bulbous eyes and munched on sea grass while the Merpeople gathered at the water's edge.

Meeshell hadn't slept a wink. How could she? So much was about to happen. Not only was she going to leave her family and travel to a new world, but she was going to change the shape of her body!

The Sea Witch parked her rather large self onto a boulder. Then she sipped a cup of briny brew. She looked as if she'd come to watch a special show. "Coral, are you ready?"

"Hold on a minute," King Philip said. "I still have some concerns about your daughter casting the spell. She's very young, after all. Can you guarantee that nothing will go wrong?"

The Sea Witch took another sip, then cackled. "Philip, my dear, you know there are no guarantees where magic is concerned." She reached into the water, pulled out a wiggling eel, and ate it whole. Then she dabbed at the corners of her mouth with a piece of kelp. "But Coral is my daughter, which means she's extremely talented and intelligent, just like me." She paused, as if waiting for Meeshell and her parents to confirm what she'd said. But they said nothing. She glowered and the air around her turned stormy. But her anger faded quickly and she took another sip. "Anyhoo, as I was saying, Coral is

perfectly capable of changing a tail into legs, aren't you, darling?"

Meeshell and her parents looked at Coral, who thus far had said nothing. She swam next to the boulder, chewing nervously on her lower lip. She was so different from her mother, quiet and with delicate features. Was she Sea Witch material? "Well, actually, I've only practiced the spell on eels—you know, since they don't have legs—and it did work but then…" She held up an eel, who glanced worriedly at the Sea Witch. "But then the legs fell off after a day."

"Fell off?" Meeshell cried, her hand flying to her mouth.

"That's alarming," Queen Pearl said.

"Oh, it's really not that bad. The eel hated having those legs." Coral let the eel go and it swam into the depths before the Sea Witch could eat it.

"I can't have legs that fall off," Meeshell said. "Dad, do something."

"Why are you asking your daddy to do something?" the Sea Witch said snippily. "He has no magic. We're the witches. Talk to *us*."

Meeshell swam closer to the Sea Witch than she'd ever been—so close that she could see the barnacles that grew on the witch's earlobes. She felt so nervous, her tail trembled. But she knew that the Sea Witch had as much to lose as she did. "It's in both our best interests that this spell work," Meeshell reminded her. "If you believe that Coral can do it, then I shall also believe. Because if this doesn't work, and I'm a failure on land, then you will never have my voice."

The water around the Sea Witch grew stormy again, and she rose onto her tail so she towered over Meeshell and her parents. "I *will* have your voice!" Her face turned as red as her tail. Even Coral swam backward, to keep clear of her mother's wrath.

While the Sea Witch was having a temper tantrum, Coral glided up to Meeshell and said, her

voice lowered, "Mom's making me do this. Just wanted you to know, in case things go wrong."

"Got it," Meeshell said. She didn't add that her mom and dad were also making her do something she didn't want to do. Why couldn't Ever After High wait for another year? There were so many fun things going on in the Merkingdom. She'd miss the next manta ray races. And her friends were planning on surfing the outer reef next week.

"Let's do this!" the Sea Witch hollered. She settled back on her boulder.

Meeshell kissed her mom and dad, trying very hard to hold back tears. They said all sorts of comforting things to her. They'd send letters. They'd send care packages. She'd have fun. She'd be home at the end of the quarter for a visit. But none of those things made Meeshell feel better. Choking back a sob, she swam into the shallows, until she was sitting in the sand. A pair of turtles waddled away, leaving a little trail of footprints.

"Go on, Coral, cast the spell. You know it by heart." The Sea Witch waved her daughter forward.

Coral, looking as if she was about to face a great white shark, slowly swam into the shallows next to Meeshell. She lifted her hands into the air. One hand held a slender wand, made from carved abalone shell. Meeshell couldn't help but notice that the hand was trembling. As Coral spoke the words that would change Meeshell's life, everyone and everything held perfectly still and in absolute silence. Even the waves halted their course.

> *"Through the power vested in me,*
> *By the wild magic sea,*
> *Two legged shall she be."*

Meeshell looked at her beautiful tail, with its blue shimmering scales. She wanted to squeeze her eyes closed, just in case something terrible happened. But she mustered her courage. Right before her eyes, her beloved tail faded away, and when she reached

out, she found not the familiar texture of scales, but something soft and smooth.

It was a leg. And right beside it was another leg. Two legs! Meeshell kicked, as she would with her tail, and the legs flopped awkwardly.

"Marvelous!" the Sea Witch cried. She began to applaud. "Well done, my dear!"

Coral smiled, just as surprised as everyone else that her spell had worked.

It took a long time for Meeshell to get to her feet, and then to keep her balance. Luckily, the sand was a soft place to fall. By the time she'd mastered walking a few steps, a ship appeared in the distance. The *Narwhal* had come to take her to Ever After High.

It had already been decided that Meeshell would hide her identity, so there were quick kisses good-bye, and words of comfort. King Philip and Queen Pearl disappeared beneath the water, as did Coral and the Sea Witch. Meeshell made her way onto the dock, her bag in hand, watching as the ship drew closer and closer.

"Oh, I forgot to tell you something." Coral popped out of the water, then floated next to the dock.

"What?" Meeshell asked.

"There's a little thing you should know about the spell."

Meeshell's entire body stiffened. "A little thing?"

"You're really lucky that you get to go to Ever After High. I hope I can go there one day. Do you think you'll meet your prince?"

"My prince?"

"The one in your story. The only one you'll give up your voice for and live with happily ever after."

Oh, *that* prince. With all the emotional upheaval of the last twenty-four hours, Meeshell hadn't thought about her future prince. He was supposed to be a land-dweller, so it was possible that he went to Ever After High.

"I don't know if I'll meet him," Meeshell said. "But, Coral, what is the little thing you forgot to tell me?"

"Oh right." She reached out of the water and pointed at Meeshell's legs. "You can't get them wet or they'll turn back into a tail. But then once the tail dries, it'll turn back into legs. See ya." And then she disappeared.

That was not a *little thing*.

A Pair of Princes

*H*ow come you're afraid of water?" Ashlynn asked. The girls were still sitting in the Castleteria.

"I'm..." Meeshell paused. *Because if my legs get wet, then they will turn back into my tail and you'll all know the truth about me.* "I'm not sure. I just am."

"Well, we all have our fears, don't we?" Apple said in an understanding way. "Actually, I've never told anyone this, but I used to be afraid of apples. When I was little, of course. Because I didn't realize that only one of them would be poisoned."

"I don't like storms," Ashlynn said. "They upset the birds, you know."

"I got bit by my horse when I was little," Briar said. "I didn't ride for three years after that."

"I prefer to be afraid of things on Fridays," Maddie said, as if this were perfectly normal. She reached into her teacup hat and pulled out a platter of tea cakes. "Oh, I almost forgot. Dad sent these over from the shoppe."

The girls each ate a tea cake. While Meeshell hadn't enjoyed the porridge, she added tea cakes to her mental list of delicious new foods. Ashlynn and Maddie hurried off to class, and just as Meeshell finished her last sip of tea, Apple said, "Oh look, here comes Daring."

Meeshell recognized the handsome prince immediately, having seen his face plastered all over the bookstore merchandise. But the surprise was that he was even better looking in person. That regal nose, that chiseled jaw, those dreamy eyes! Meeshell's heart skipped a beat.

"Hello, ladies." He swept a plate aside and sat on the corner of the table. And then he smiled. Briar Beauty quickly slid her crownglasses into place, then threw her hands over Meeshell's eyes.

"You can't look directly at him when he does that," she informed her. "His smile is so bright that if you look at his teeth, you'll see spots for days."

Good to know.

As soon as the light faded, Briar removed her hands. Meeshell stole a shy glance, then quickly looked away as her heart skipped another beat.

Apple made the introductions. "Meeshell, this is Daring Charming. Daring, this is our newest student, Meeshell. She comes from the Kingdom by the Sea."

"H-h-hello," Meeshell stammered.

Daring pushed his thick blond hair off his forehead. "No need to say it. I know you're enchanted to make my acquaintance." He whipped out a photo from his pocket and handed it to her. "It's already signed."

She looked at the photo.

It was inscribed:

To my loyal fan, from the prince you adore,
Daring Charming. xoxo

"You're welcome," he said.

Seriously? Meeshell's heart stopped skipping beats. Yes, he was eye candy, but he was way too full of himself. She knew boys exactly like him back home. He was definitely not her type. She politely tucked the picture into her book bag. He took a long look in a nearby mirror, then strode away. Briar

slid her crownglasses back onto her forehead. "You'll get used to him," she said.

Apple neatly folded her paper tea cake holder and set it aside. "Daring might spend a lot of time talking about himself, but he kind of can't help it. I mean, he's spent his whole life knowing that he's destined to become Prince Charming. That can give a guy a healthy ego!"

Meeshell watched as Daring sauntered from the Castleteria, catching eager glances from girls along the way. He stopped two more times to check his reflection. She remembered Coral's question. Would she meet her future prince at Ever After High? If so, she hoped they wouldn't all be like Daring. She had no idea how to relate to a guy like that. She wanted someone who didn't care so much about how he looked. Someone who liked to talk about interesting things.

Someone smart.

Apple waved. "Hey, Humphrey, can you come

over here for a moment? I'd like you to meet our new student."

Another boy walked toward the table. From first glance, the only thing he had in common with Daring Charming, physically, was that a crown sat on his head. He was of average height and average build. He wore a button-down shirt, suspenders, and bow tie. He didn't walk as if he owned the world. Rather, he seemed hesitant to approach the table. No girls sighed as he passed by.

"Humphrey, this is Meeshell. She's a new student and she's not familiar with MirrorPads so she's going to need your help signing into the network, etcetera." She turned to Meeshell. "Humphrey Dumpty is the president of the Tech Club, so any tech troubles you have, he'll know how to solve them."

"Uh, hi," Humphrey said. He made eye contact for only a moment, which was fine with Meeshell because she was starting to feel overwhelmed by all the introductions. He shuffled in place. "So, yeah,

uh, I'm always happy to help. But right now I have a Tech Club meeting. Can I help you later?"

"Sure," Meeshell said.

"Okay." He fiddled with a collection of pens and pencils that were crammed into his shirt pocket. "I'll see you later." Then he hurried away, but just before he reached the exit, his foot met a chair leg and he stumbled forward. *"Ahhh!"* he cried, his arms reaching to break his fall. As he tumbled onto the floor, the few students who were still lingering in the Castleteria gasped with alarm. Meeshell stared at Humphrey, who was now sprawled, facedown, on the Castleteria floor. But before anyone could move to help him, he scrambled back to his feet. "I'm fine, I'm fine," he said, brushing off some toast crumbs. Then he used both hands to feel all over his head. "Yeah, I'm definitely fine. No cracks. It's all good." He cast an embarrassed glance at Meeshell, then exited.

Oh, he was from *that* Dumpty family.

Thus far, Meeshell had met two very different princes. She hoped that somewhere in between the overly confident hero who handed out signed pictures of himself and the shy, clumsy guy who'd barely spoken to her, there'd be a normal prince for her.

*T*he next thing on the Welcoming Committee to-do list was: *Check New Student into a Dormitory Room.*

The girls' dormitory and the boys' dormitory were separated by a large Common Room, where the students spent lots of time socializing, doing throne-work, and sometimes just relaxing in front of the river-rock fireplace. Getting to the dorm room required climbing more staircases. Meeshell's legs began to ache. She felt envious of the fairy students,

who zipped past, their wings leaving cool breezes in their wake. "I know," Apple said, as if reading her mind. "If only we had wings."

They stopped at room 12C. The sign on the door read:

FARRAH GOODFAIRY AND MEESHELL

The words twinkled. Apple knocked gently. The door flew open and a girl with blue hair and large blue eyes stood before them. "You must be Meeshell," she said with a big, welcoming hug. "I'm so happy to finally get a roommate. Come on in." When she flew around, Meeshell realized that her roommate was a fairy. How hexciting!

The room was a good size, with two canopied beds, two desks, two dressers, and two closets. This fairy clearly had a favorite color because the bedspreads, pillows, overstuffed chairs, and paint were all variations of blue. "These boxes arrived for you

from the Glass Slipper." Three shoe boxes sat on Meeshell's bed. She set her MirrorPad and book bag next to them. "Where are the rest of your things?" Farrah asked.

"Yes, I was wondering the same thing," Apple said. "Why haven't the trolls delivered your luggage? I could call my dwarf network. They do a great job with deliveries."

"This is all I have for now. My mom ordered some new clothes for me, but I guess they haven't arrived," Meeshell explained.

"Oh, that's no problem. Farrah happens to be a future fairy godmother, so I'm sure she can help you if you need an outfit."

"Yes, of course. What do you need? How about a jacket?"

She grabbed a silver wand from her vanity and waved it through the air. A little trail of sparkles appeared. Suddenly, Meeshell was wearing a cropped jacket that perfectly matched her dress.

"Thank you," Meeshell said gratefully.

"Just so you know, my spells don't last very long. That jacket will disappear at midnight."

It would seem that Farrah, a future fairy godmother, and Coral, a future sea witch, had something in common—their spells had glitches.

Meeshell opened the shoe boxes. Then she sat on the bed and began trying them on.

Farrah pulled Apple aside. Even though Farrah had lowered her voice to a whisper, Meeshell could still hear the muffled conversation. "How come she speaks so quietly? Is she shy?" Farrah asked Apple.

"Well, she does have a sore throat. But yes, she's very shy. I bet she's homesick, too. I think it might take a while for her to feel comfortable with us."

"Oh, I remember feeling that way when school started."

"Me too. But I'm her Welcoming Committee representative, so I'll do everything I can to help her settle in."

89

"Hi!" three voices called.

Ashlynn, Briar, and Maddie all walked into the dorm room. "Oh look, the shoes arrived. Those are adorable." Ashlynn pointed to the pink sneakers that Meeshell had on her feet. These were the ones she found the most comfortable. Ashlynn held a vase, with a strange-looking flower. "We thought maybe we got off on the wrong slipper so we brought you this flower for your dorm."

"It's a snapdragon," Briar said.

Meeshell had never seen a snapdragon before—they didn't grow under the sea. The flower was pretty, with large petals that folded over one another. But when Meeshell leaned forward to smell the flower, the petals unfurled and a cute little dragon face appeared. It opened its mouth and roared at her! Ashlynn laughed as the vase shook in her hands, spilling some water.

Meeshell jumped away. Luckily, the water missed her, landing on the floor instead.

"Oops," Ashlynn said. "Sorry about that." The

little dragon flower began to snap its mouth at her. "I'll just put it over here." Ashlynn set the flower next to Meeshell's bed.

Meeshell wondered if the little dragon would move around during the night. What if it splashed water on her while she was sleeping and her tail came out for her roommate to see? "Is it...safe?" she asked nervously.

"Oh, never mind, you don't have to keep it," Ashlynn said quickly, picking the flower up. "I didn't know you were afraid of snapdragons! Or is it the water? Are you afraid of flower water, too?"

I'm not really afraid of cute little flowers...or water! she wanted to explain. *I just can't get my legs wet.* The girls were looking at her, waiting for her to say something.

Apple sensed her discomfort and jumped in to try to help her new friend. "You don't have to explain." She grabbed a towel from the bathroom and mopped up the spill. Then she began to usher everyone from the room. "I think we should give Meeshell some

time to herself. It's been a long day, and she's probably tired." She motioned to Farrah, who followed her into the hallway. Then Apple poked her head back into the room. "We'll let you rest. And I'm going to get you some lozenges for your throat. See you soon." And with that, she gently closed the door. Meeshell overheard their conversation as they walked away.

"I don't think I've ever met someone so shy before," Briar said.

Then Maddie said, "I'm pretty sure it's my hat. She doesn't like my hat."

Their voices faded, leaving Meeshell alone for the first time since arriving.

It was a relief to be alone. She sank onto the bed and let the soft pillow cradle her head.

So many feelings swirled inside her. Everyone had been so nice, and they clearly thought she was a two-footed land-dweller, just like them. But now they thought she had some kind of phobia of water—*all* water. What if she got thirsty and needed

a drink? What would she do? How silly it was—a mermaid pretending to be afraid of water.

She rose from the bed, then walked onto the balcony, looking out over the campus. Students mingled in the quad. Swans swam around the unicorn fountain. A forest spread to the south and the sea spread to the east. There was no sign of the *Narwhal*. How she longed to be back on that ship, heading home. Back to the watery world she loved. Back to her family and friends.

Back to her beloved tail.

A chime sounded somewhere nearby, pulling Meeshell from her musings. She turned and walked back into the dorm room. The chime sounded again. Was it coming from the MirrorPad? She picked it up. The screen lit up.

Welcome to the Ever After High Mirror Network. You have a message from StoryTeller2. To respond to your message, please set up your Mirror Network chat room account.

A keypad appeared, asking her to fill in her code name for access to the chat room. She sat on the bed and thought a moment. What type of code name should she choose? The answer came quickly. She typed **Seashell**.

> Welcome to the Mirror Network chat room.
> New message from StoryTeller2.
> **StoryTeller2**: Hi.

Because they didn't have MirrorPads in her kingdom, using her fingers to type was as difficult as using her feet to walk, so it took a while to get the hang of it. But soon she mastered the two-finger method.

> **Seashell**: Hi.
> **StoryTeller2**: How are you doing?
> **Seashell**: Fine. Who is this?
> **StoryTeller2**: I'm a student. I know what it's like to be the new kid. It's overwhelming at

first. If you have any questions about school,
I'm happy to answer.

Seashell: Thanks.

There was a long pause. Meeshell wasn't sure what to do. Was it rude if she didn't ask questions? How did this work?

StoryTeller2: Okay, well, I'm here if you need me. Bye.

Seashell: Bye.

The screen went dark. She sat back against the headboard. What an odd way to talk to someone. She didn't know who StoryTeller2 was, but he or she seemed very nice. And apparently, he or she knew her. Had they already met?

The sound of beating wings drew Meeshell's attention to the open balcony door. Four tiny fairies flew into the room, leaving trails of sparkles in the air. They carried an enormous package, which they

dropped onto the bed. The label read: *From Fashionably Ever After...For Meeshell.*

"Thank you," Meeshell told the little creatures, amazed they could carry such weight. They all zipped away.

She eagerly untied the twine and opened the package. A note inside read:

Dear Meeshell,

I loved Fashionably Ever After when I lived on land. They always provided me with the loveliest outfits. Hope you enjoy these.

Hugs and kisses,
Mom

Meeshell opened the box. It was stuffed with clothing—dresses, pants, tops, pajamas, and a swimsuit. Well, the swimsuit wouldn't be needed, since she couldn't get her legs wet. She set that into a

drawer, along with the pants and shirts. She hung the dresses in her closet. Then she opened her bag and took out her precious belongings—a brush and comb, seashell clips for her hair, a princess mermaid arm bracelet, her pearl headband, and her favorite pink coral necklace.

"Oh, that's gorgeous!" Apple said when she returned with lozenges. She was referring to an asymmetrical dress with lightweight ruffles, which looked, to Meeshell, like waves. The dress had a coral top with scalloped fish-skin texture. "And this is adorable!" Apple pulled a teal sea-horse-shaped purse from the Fashionably Ever After box. Then she smiled. "It's kinda funny that you're afraid of water but you have a total sea theme going here with your clothes."

"Yeah, that is funny," Meeshell said sheepishly.

"I hope these work." Apple gave Meeshell the box of pickled pepper throat lozenges.

"Thanks. Me too." While her feet were content in their new sneakers, her throat was feeling more

ragged than ever. She didn't want to think about what would happen if her voice didn't recover. She popped one of the lozenges into her mouth. Then, for good measure, added another. She nearly gagged. They tasted disgusting!

"I know you're feeling a bit overwhelmed," Apple said, "but tomorrow will be great. It's Club Day. That means you can walk around and check out all the clubs until you find one or two to join. Or three. There's no limit. One quarter, I joined twenty-two clubs. Was I ever busy! But you do whatever works for you. And I'll be there so you don't have to worry about getting lost. It will be spelltacular."

Meeshell hoped so.

Becoming a land-dweller was her destiny and she wanted to make the best of it. She hoped the lozenges would work. Because it didn't matter if she had no shoes, or if she wore the same yellow dress for the rest of her life. What mattered was her voice.

It needed to heal because it was the key to her future.

Above
the Waves

It is a well-known fact that Merpeople love to sing. Their vocal cords are uniquely designed to produce sounds that travel underwater.

In Meeshell's kingdom, Merchoirs existed for every age group, and while not everyone joined, everyone could sing. And sing well. So while under the water, Meeshell's voice sounded similar to the other mermaid voices—perfectly in tune and fluid like the water itself. And like her friends, she mastered many sea-creature languages, which required a variety of sounds that human vocal cords cannot produce. So even though she was a princess, when Meeshell sang in the kelp grotto with her friends, she was simply a member of a choir, equal in tonality and harmony.

However, when Meeshell surfaced, which Merpeople often do, her voice changed in a unique way. It sounded...*human*. According to the Sea Witch, an avid collector of voices, Meeshell's above-water voice was magnificent. Breathtaking. The most beautiful voice the Sea Witch had ever heard. It was something to be coveted.

But none of the other Merpeople seemed impressed with this discovery. It was tradition to sing underwater, and that is where they made most of their music. So the fact that Meeshell sounded human above the water did not cause a commotion. Except with the Sea Witch.

"Why does your mom collect voices?" Meeshell asked Coral one day. Coral often swam behind

Meeshell and her friends, never joining in, but always there, watching.

"She hates her own voice," Coral said. There was good reason. The Sea Witch, who was only part mermaid, had a voice dark as a storm and prickly as a sea urchin. "So she likes to try on other voices, like trying on a new hat. Your mom's was once her favorite."

The Sea Witch had possessed Queen Pearl's voice, but only for a short time. That changed when the story went in another direction and Prince Philip fell in love with his Little Mermaid and agreed to live below the waves with her.

"True love always breaks spells," Coral said. She looked slyly at Meeshell. "Do you know why my mom wants *your* voice?"

"She likes the way it sounds," Meeshell said simply. Everyone knew that.

"Yes, but that's not the only reason." Coral swam a little closer. "Mom told me that she's sick of being the Sea Witch. She wants to become a famous singer and travel the world. She thinks your voice will make that happen for her."

"Really?" Meeshell tried to imagine the Sea Witch living on land, traveling from town to town, putting on concerts. Would someone have to push her around in a tank of water? Or would she be able to magic herself a pair of legs?

Coral and Meeshell swam under a coral arch. "My only regret about being half Sea Witch is that I inherited my mom's bad voice."

"No, you didn't," Meeshell said honestly. "Your voice is nice."

Coral laughed. "Nice? Have you ever heard me sing?" Meeshell shook her head. Come to think of it, Coral had never participated in any of the choirs. "I'm terrible. The worst!"

"You can't be that bad," Meeshell said.

"You wanna bet?"

They swam to the surface. It was a calm afternoon. The water was as smooth as glass. Coral swam

to a reef and sat on a rock. She opened her mouth and…

That wasn't singing!

Meeshell's fingers flew to her ears. The sounds coming from Coral's mouth were unlike anything Meeshell had ever heard. The noise started out screechier than a gull, then dipped deeper than a seal's bark. "Okay, okay," Meeshell said. "Stop. Please stop."

Coral closed her mouth. Then she laughed. "I told you so."

Meeshell climbed onto the rock next to her. "Do you think your mom might give my voice to you instead?" Meeshell brightened at that idea. To give up her voice was a sacrifice she'd been born to make, but to give it to the nasty Sea Witch had always seemed unfair. Giving it to Coral, a nice girl who'd never done anything mean to anyone in the ocean, seemed much more palatable.

"That's a nice idea, but Mom definitely wants your voice for herself. Besides, I don't care about singing. It's totally not my thing." She dipped her hand into the water and scooped out a little fish. Meeshell cringed, wondering if Coral would eat the fish whole, just like the Sea Witch always did. But Coral got a dreamy look on her face, then released the little creature. "If Mom becomes a famous singer and leaves the ocean, that means that I'll take her place as the Sea Witch, and you know what I'm going to do with all that power?"

"What?"

Coral sighed, her shoulders slumped. "Drat. I thought you'd have a good suggestion. I'm not really sure what I want to do."

"That's okay," Meeshell said. "We have a long time before we have to make those big decisions about our lives."

As they sat on the rock, looking out over the water, both girls knew that destiny was at work. Coral's magic would get stronger. And Meeshell's voice would not always belong to her.

A chime sounded. Meeshell opened her eyes and rolled over in bed. It took her a moment to remember where she was. Then the chime sounded again. The noise was coming from her MirrorPad. She reached out, grabbed it, and read the screen.

Good morning. Time to get up.

Apple had set the alarm for her. How odd to wake up in a bed that was surrounded by air. And

stranger still, to be covered in so many blankets. Usually, the first thing she did after waking was to feed Finbert. Then she would swim into the dining room to have breakfast with her parents. But she had no idea how her mornings would go at Ever After High.

She sat up. A note lay on her bedside table. It was from Farrah. *I had to leave hextra early this morning to help set up the Fairy Club booth. See you later.* Meeshell was surprised she hadn't heard Farrah getting ready. She must have slept like a sea log, as her mom would say. She stretched out her arms and yawned. Then she stretched her tail, but when two feet popped out the end of the blanket she nearly shrieked. She pulled back the covers.

Right. She'd momentarily forgotten about those two things.

Her MirrorPad chimed again.

New Message from StoryTeller2.

StoryTeller2: Good morning.

Seashell: Hi.

StoryTeller2: Did you know that today is Club Day?

Seashell: Yes. I'm supposed to find a club to join.

StoryTeller2: I hope you find something that you really like.

Oh, how nice, she thought.

Seashell: Will you be there?

StoryTeller2: Yes. Oops, I mean, maybe.

Seashell: Since you know who I am, will you introduce yourself to me?

Super-long pause.

StoryTeller2: I gotta go. Good luck today.

Meeshell frowned. It was so odd not to know who was on the other side of the conversation. Was this

normal on land? Did people often hide their identities and talk to one another?

A knock sounded on the door. "It's just me," a familiar voice called. Apple entered the room, as cheerful as ever. She wore a lovely red dress. A pair of bluebirds was tying a ribbon in her hair. "How's your voice?" she asked.

Meeshell hadn't spoken a word since waking, so she didn't know the answer. And she was a bit afraid to find out—partly because of what it might mean to her story, but also because she didn't want to eat any more of those horrid pickled pepper lozenges. She put a hand protectively to her throat. "I...I'm not sure." Then she smiled. Her voice sounded quite normal. What a relief! "I guess it's better."

"It sounds spelltacular! Those lozenges must have done the trick."

Perhaps it had been the lozenges, or, as Professor Yaga had said, maybe her vocal cords had needed time to get used to being in the air 24/7. While Apple waited, Meeshell went into the bathroom and changed into one of her new outfits that her mom had sent. When she emerged, Apple laughed, but not in a mean way. "How come you're wearing pajamas?"

Meeshell looked down at the pants and top, both made from soft cotton and covered with little sea horse designs. She tried to play it cool. "Uh, well, we sometimes wear pajamas back home. Don't you do that here?"

"Only on Pajama Day." Apple sat on Meeshell's bed. The bluebirds had flown away, but a pair of yellow songbirds was running a comb through Apple's hair. "But today isn't Pajama Day. It's Club Day. All the clubs on campus will have booths set up in the quad and they'll be looking for new members. This is the perfect opportunity for you to find the perfect club. Or two. Or three. Go ahead and change, and I'll go with you."

Meeshell appreciated how patient Apple was being with her, but she didn't want to take advantage of her kindness. "Oh, you don't have to keep being my Welcoming Committee. You must have more important things to do."

Apple laughed again. "Nothing is more important than doing my duty. And right now, that is to find you a club." She held up her Welcoming Committee list. "It's the last thing on the list."

"Oh, okay. Thanks."

Meeshell picked another outfit from her closet. This dress was similar to the one she'd worn the day before, with a scalloped texture and with ruffles along the hem that looked like waves. She held it up, and received an approving nod from Apple. Then she went back into the bathroom. She stood in front of the mirror, staring at her reflection, but not in the way that Daring admired his. Rather, she felt as if she was looking at a stranger. *Who are you?* she asked herself. Who is this land-dweller, standing in a dorm room, with two feet, attending the most prestigious school in all the kingdoms? Her parents were expecting her to do her best, which meant getting good grades and making new friends. And if that wasn't enough to cause one's scales to tremble, she'd be trying to get those grades and friends while hiding her true identity as a mermaid. How would she pull this off? She leaned against the wall, her chest tight, her breathing quick. Suddenly, she felt as if she'd been tangled in a fisherman's net!

"Meeshell? You okay?" Apple asked gently from the other side of the door.

"Yes. I'm almost ready." Meeshell told herself to snap out of it. The good news was that her speaking voice was back to normal. Did that mean her singing voice was back, too? She'd have to find a safe, private place to give it a try. In the meantime, she should stop worrying so much and brave the day. It was all going to work out. She was going to live her destiny!

After dressing, Meeshell arranged her pearl headband and chose a lovely statement necklace that sparkled with shells and coral. Then she grabbed her MirrorPad and sea horse purse, and followed Apple.

Walking down one flight of stairs, then another and another, was much easier than it had been yesterday, which was a very good sign that she was getting used to her legs. And when she and Apple stepped into the quad, they were greeted by a chorus of "hellos," which was a very good sign that the other students were getting used to Meeshell. Apple stopped at a coffee cart and got them each a mocha frappé, which Meeshell loved. "Can I have one of these every morning?"

"Sure, if you want. The cart is from the Hocus Latte Café in the village. You can get all sorts of drinks there, too."

The world was full of so many new flavors. As she sipped the chocolaty goodness, birds sang in the branches above. A dragon glided over distant tree-tops. A boy and that rabbit she'd seen with the glasses walked past, both their noses stuck in books. The boy was quite handsome, and wearing a crown. Then she saw two more boys with crowns. Wow, there sure were a lot of princes at this school.

Was one of them destined to be part of her story? Maybe the one who was currently staring at her?

"Whassup, ladies?" he called. He had piercing green eyes and freckles. He was dressed in khaki shorts, a velvet jacket, and bow tie.

Apple, once again, made the introductions. "Meeshell, this is Hopper Croakington II. Hopper, this is our newest student, Meeshell."

Hopper wagged his eyebrows at her. "Well, hello. You can be *me* shell anytime." Meeshell wasn't sure what that meant but she smiled politely. Was he trying to flirt with her? He leaned against a tree. "What brings you to—?" He turned suddenly. "Briar," he whispered. Briar Beauty was walking across the quad. She waved at Apple and Meeshell, and at Hopper. A blush spread across his face and…

Poof!

Meeshell looked down at the ground. Where Hopper had once stood, there was now a green frog. The frog adjusted his little gold crown, looked up at her, and said, "Delighted to make your

acquaintance. If you ever find yourself in need of companionship, I am a skilled conversationalist. Good day." He bowed, then hurried away on his little bowlegged green legs.

How odd. Meeshell was about to ask Apple what was up with this Hopper guy, when she saw another boy with a crown. She'd met him yesterday in the Castleteria. What was his name? Oh yes, Humphrey.

He was carrying a stack of MirrorPads. He noticed her looking at him and stopped walking. His face turned red. He fiddled with his bow tie, waved, then backed into a hedge, landing on his rump. "I'm okay," he called as he jumped to his feet. He collected all the MirrorPads. "Nothing cracked!" Then he hurried away.

She hadn't meant to stare at him. Poor guy. Was it possible that he and Meeshell were equally shy? And equally awkward?

The far side of the quad was crowded with white tents. A sign was posted on each tent:

PEGASUS-RIDING CLUB

WAND-MAKING CLUB

FAIRY CLUB

Representatives for each club sat at tables that were piled with informational brochures. Apple and Meeshell walked between the tents, with Apple stopping to give Meeshell a brief description of each club. "And that's the Oversleepers Anonymous Club." Briar sat inside that tent, her chin resting in her hands.

"There's no shame in being sleepy," Briar called out. "Join today and get a free pair of wide-awake glasses so you can fall asleep in class without being caught." The glasses were lined up on the table. Each had a pair of eyes painted on the front—wide-awake eyes that blinked occasionally.

Farrah was tending to the Fairy Club booth, which was covered in so much fairy dust, passersby started sneezing.

Ashlynn and Maddie walked up. "Hi, Meeshell," they both said.

"Hi."

"Hey, you're not whispering anymore," Ashlynn noted with a smile.

"My sore throat is gone."

"I'm helping Meeshell pick a club to join," Apple explained. "Do you have any suggestions?"

"I'm in the Forest Club," Ashlynn said. "We sweep the forest floor to keep it nice and tidy. If you joined, we could sweep together."

"I'm in the Wonderland Club," Maddie said. "It's supposed to be for people from Wonderland. But most people get to Wonderland by mistake, so it doesn't seem fair to say just because you haven't fallen down a rabbit hole, you can't join. So we let anyone join. Do you speak Riddlish? That helps. It's our club's language."

"I really like the Library Club," Apple said. "We don't do much, just study together. It really helps me keep my grades up. Oh, and you could always join Daring's fan club." They'd stopped at the Daring Charming Fan Club tent. Five girls and one guy sat at a table covered in Daring Charming memorabilia. And right next to it was the Tech Club. Humphrey sat at a table covered in all sorts of gadgets. He looked away when Meeshell looked at him. *Yep*, she thought. *Painfully shy.* She wondered if there was a Shy Club they could both join.

None of the suggested clubs sounded like the right fit to Meeshell. She was about to move to the next tent when a mirror on a nearby tree lit up. A girl with blond curls appeared in the mirror. Her curls bobbed as she talked. "Hello, fellow fairytales! Blondie Lockes here to give you the latest scoop. I'm happy to announce that we have a new student. She arrived by boat yesterday, from the faraway Kingdom by the Sea. Her name is Meeshell and she's rooming with Farrah Goodfairy, and from what

I've heard, they are getting along swimmingly. So please give her a big Ever After High welcome." All the students who were hanging out in the quad turned toward Meeshell and clapped. Meeshell wasn't sure what to do. She gave a little wave, then tried to disappear in the shadows beneath one of the tents. Blondie whispered to someone offscreen, then looked back into the camera. "In other news, it's just been confirmed that our very own glee club, the Happily-Glees, are going to give an impromptu performance in the quad right now. They will be performing a brand-new song directed by our very own Melody Piper."

A glee club? Meeshell stepped out from the shadows. Maybe this could be the club she joined.

Six singers gathered beneath an oak tree. A girl with a pair of headphones stood before them. "That's Melody," Apple whispered in Meeshell's ear. Melody clearly loved music because she was adorned with musical notes—on her leather vest, her silver tights, and on her black leather booties. She took a pitch

pipe from her pocket and blew a single note. Each of the singers hummed, trying to match the note. Melody shook her head, then blew on the pipe again. The singers hummed again. Melody's shoulders slumped. No one had found the note. Meeshell frowned. That wasn't a good sign.

Melody raised her hands and the Happily-Glees began to sing.

> *"Looking for my ever after*
> *Don't wanna see my dreams get*
> *shattered*
> *Everybody says I have to, got to,*
> *Wait around just to be rescued.*
> *Not gonna sit alone in a tower.*
> *I'll show the world my princess power.*
> *I'm standing up 'cause I am stronger.*
> *Listen to my heart; it's getting louder."*

It was…terrible. Not the song—the song itself was great. The lyrics were brilliant. But the singing

was…well, it was like listening to a pod of elephant seals. Okay, maybe not *that* bad, but Meeshell was used to Mer-singing, the most beautiful singing in all the kingdoms. She winced, then tried to force a smile. Perhaps she was being overly critical. Perhaps this was considered good singing in the land-dwelling world. She glanced at Apple. The fairest-in-the-land princess was also trying very hard not to wince, but a tiny scowl had formed between her eyebrows. So it was true—they *were* terrible.

One of the singers was clearly off-key, while another singer was way too loud. The harmony wasn't working, and the choreography, well, it was just a mess.

When the song finished, everyone smiled and politely applauded, then went on about their business. The singers ambled off and Melody lingered, her expression one of frustration. Apple tried to console her. "That was really…interesting," Apple said.

"It's not supposed to sound like that," Melody explained. "There were a lot of wrong notes."

Maddie giggled. "I thought it was tea-rriffic. In Wonderland, the wrong notes are always the right notes."

Melody sighed. "We really need more practice time. And we could really use new members."

Apple's eyes lit up. "Hey, Meeshell is looking for a club to join."

Melody looked hopefully at Meeshell. "Do you sing?" she asked.

Meeshell wanted to shout *Yes! Yes, I sing! I love singing.* But now that she'd heard these singers, she realized that if she sang with them, her voice would totally stand out. If she joined the Happily-Glees, surely someone would figure out her true identity, for her voice was even more famous than her tail. She sighed with disappointment. This was the one club she truly wanted to join, but she'd have to pass. "No," she said. "I can't carry a tune."

"That's too bad. We really need a soloist. Your speaking voice is so pretty I would've bet you could sing beautifully. Well, see you all later." Melody set her headphones back over her ears and headed toward the coffee cart.

"Don't fret," Apple said. "Something will pop up. It always does." At that, a mouse popped out of Maddie's teacup hat and squeaked.

"Tomorrow is Sports Day," Ashlynn said. "Maybe you can try out for a team. I'm on the cheerhexing squad. Maybe you'd like to join?"

"That's a spelltacular idea," Apple told her. "All the teams will be having tryouts, and my Welcoming Committee list says I'm supposed to get you signed up for at least one club or sports team. Tomorrow is a new day! We can still make this work!"

Down the Drain

It had been a long day. Meeshell felt a bit of a failure, having chosen no clubs. And while classes had gone okay, she'd been too shy to speak up in any of them. And during dinner, there'd been so many new faces and introductions, her head was swimming. When she got back to the dormitory, she overheard a conversation in the hallway. It was Apple and Briar.

"I don't think I'm right for the Welcoming Committee," Apple said to Briar.

"Why?"

"I haven't been able to help Meeshell find a club."

"Well, helping the new student find some sort of activity is really important, that's true. And the Welcoming Committee does have a one hundred percent success rate."

"One hundred percent?" Apple gulped. "You mean, I could mess that up? That would be an epic fairy fail."

"You won't mess it up. You're Apple White. You can do anything you"—Briar paused for a huge yawn—"anything you set your mind to."

"Thanks for the vote of confidence," Apple said. "I'll keep trying. Meeshell deserves to feel like she belongs. We all do."

Just as the conversation ended, Professor Yaga called Meeshell on her MirrorPad and was happy to hear that her speaking voice had returned to normal. And that her legs were working better and hadn't fallen off, which was a real plus! "Remember,

if you have any unusual symptoms or concerns, call me immediately. Otherwise, how are things going?"

"Fine." Her answer didn't sound very convincing.

"I hear homesickness in your voice. It might be worse for you than for others since you are hiding your true nature," Professor Yaga said. Luckily, Meeshell was alone in her dorm room, which meant that no one overheard the conversation. "My advice to you is, whenever you are able, let your true self out. Otherwise, you'll always feel like a fish out of water." The MirrorPad screen went dark as the call ended.

Yes, that's exactly how she felt. What a perfect description. She wanted, very badly, to let her true self out. To see her tail again. That would make her feel better.

She stepped into the bathroom. Unfortunately, there was no bathtub. The shower was pretty, however, made of pink tiles and a unicorn faucet. It would have to do. She locked the door and turned on the water. When she entered the shower, the change was immediate. Her legs disappeared and her beautiful tail took its rightful place. She leaned against the wall. It was an awkward space, difficult to get comfortable in since tails are not designed for long periods of standing. She showered as best she could, but got wedged a few times in the process. This wasn't making her feel better. She turned off the water and watched it swirl down the drain.

She dried her tail with a towel and as soon as the last droplet had evaporated, her legs reappeared. It was nice to know that she could bring her tail back whenever she wanted. She was grateful to Coral for that glitch in the spell. But still she felt anxious. With all her heart, she wanted to swim. Spending day after day not swimming was like asking a seagull to stop flying. Maybe she could find a way to swim without anyone seeing?

After changing into her new pajamas, she sat on her bed, opened her MirrorPad, and searched for a

campus map. Then she perused the map, looking for large bodies of water. There was Mirror Beach, near the boat dock, but that was too exposed. There was the unicorn fountain, where the swans swam, but that was smack in the middle of the quad. There was a swimming pool in the Grimmnasium, but someone might see her there. She was about to give up when she noticed a small lake at the far edge of campus. Enchanted Lake. That sounded perfect! According to the map, she could easily walk there.

Farrah came back. She brought a late-night snack of toast and fairyberry jam, which she shared. Then she went to change into her pajamas. When she emerged from the bathroom she asked, "How did your day go?"

"Pretty good," Meeshell said.

"I'm glad to hear that." Then Farrah's gaze fell upon a fat hextbook. "Ugh, I have to study for a test tomorrow in Magicology. It's about the history of evil witches, my least favorite topic." She lugged the hextbook onto

her desk with a big thud. Then she sat and, using her wand as a highlighting pen, began to study.

Just then, Meeshell's MirrorPad chimed.

StoryTeller2: Hi.

Seashell: Hi.

StoryTeller2: How did Club Day go? Did you join anything?

Seashell: No. I didn't find anything that seemed right for me.

StoryTeller2: Yeah, I get that. When I first came to school, I couldn't find the right club, either, so I started my own.

Seashell: Really? You can do that?

StoryTeller2: Sure.

Seashell: Which club did you start?

Long pause.

StoryTeller2: Well, I gotta go. I need to do something. Talk to you later. Bye.

Seashell: Bye.

Every time she tried to find out any details about the mysterious StoryTeller2, he or she stopped chatting. Why?

As the chat box closed, the Ever After High campus map reappeared on the MirrorPad screen. StoryTeller2 wasn't the only one who needed to do something. Meeshell looked out the window.

She needed to swim!

After changing into her new bathing suit, then covering up with a coat, Meeshell told Farrah that she was going to take a walk. As she made her way down the hall, she stepped over a hedgehog who was waddling along at a leisurely pace. The Common Room was empty, except for a girl sitting in front of the fireplace, a book nestled on her lap. The girl looked up at her. "Did anyone tell you about curfew?" she asked.

Meeshell halted. "Curfew?"

The girl set a bookmark in place, then closed the book. She had lovely dark hair and matching dark eyes. Her dress was black and purple with silver lacework at the edges. "If you leave campus, you need to be back by midnight or you won't be able to pass through the wall of thorns. It's a magical wall that Headmaster Grimm uses to protect the school." She glanced up at the wall clock. "You have an hour."

"Okay, thanks for the warning."

"Don't worry, I'm not going to ask what you're doing," she said, which was a huge relief to Meeshell. "By the way, I'm Raven Queen, daughter of the Evil Queen," she added with a wry smile.

Meeshell's shoulders stiffened. Daughter of the *Evil Queen*? Wow! Of course she'd heard about Raven. *Everyone* had heard about Raven. She was as famous as Apple.

Raven waited patiently for Meeshell to introduce herself. "I'm Meeshell. Daughter of..." She paused.

Raven raised an eyebrow. When no answer came, Raven sat back in her chair. "You don't have to tell

me. I get it. Sometimes it's nice if people just know us for ourselves and not for our families." She picked up her book and started reading again. "Good luck with whatever after you're doing."

"Thank you." Meeshell hurried down the stairs. Just from that short encounter, she got the feeling that Raven was much nicer than her family's reputation.

She only had an hour to swim and get back. Would that be enough time? She didn't want to get into trouble; that was not the best way to start her first week. Behind her, the dormitory windows shone brightly against the twilight sky. Most students were studying or getting ready for bed. Was she the only student out and about? She hesitated, but the need to swim was stronger than her fear of getting caught. She gripped her bag. She'd stuffed a towel inside. And onward she went.

She crossed the quad, then a footbridge, passing a sign that read:

THIS WAY TO THE EVER AFTER HIGH SWAMP

She hadn't noticed that on the map. Swimming in a swamp didn't sound like much fun, but she'd keep it in mind as a last resort. Soon she came to another sign:

THIS WAY TO ENCHANTED LAKE

The path was narrow but well groomed, with broom marks in the wood chips. Ashlynn's Forest Club did a lovely job. The path was also well lit, thanks to the full moon. Even though Meeshell wasn't breaking any rules, she felt nervous as she walked. *I'm not doing anything wrong,* she told herself. *This is my nature. I need to swim.*

An unsettling thought popped into her head. Once she became a permanent land-dweller, would she lose her craving for the water? How odd that would be.

After a few twists and turns, the path opened onto a clearing. Tall willow trees grew around the perimeter and in the center was a small lake with water so blue, it had to be enchanted. The moon reflected on the lake's surface. The only movement came from a pair of golden cranes who stood in the shallows, between large lily pads. They turned and nodded at Meeshell, not seeming upset by her arrival. She knelt and touched the water. It was perfect: not too warm, not too cool. Her toes wiggled excitedly, as if they were really looking forward to turning into a tail. She tossed her coat aside, adjusted her bathing suit straps, and dived in.

Water! How glorious! She kicked once, twice, and her legs became a tail. Joy flowed through her as she swam beneath the surface. Then she leaped from the water, flipping into a forward roll. She leaped again, this time soaring through the air in a backward arc. Oh, the freedom! She swam the entire circumference of the lagoon, around and around until she was breathless. The cranes watched with curiosity. Then she floated on her back, looking up at the twilight sky, the water cradling her. All was still. All was good.

The cranes made a sudden screeching sound. They twisted their long necks, staring warily at the path. Footsteps. Someone was coming! Meeshell sank until her shoulders were under the water, then she slipped into a shadowy place beneath the boughs of a weeping willow.

A person appeared around the corner. It was Humphrey. What was he doing out here? He wore a pair of checkered swim shorts and little flotation devices around his arms. Meeshell had seen kids wearing those on beaches. He stood at the edge of the lagoon, staring at the water. "You can do this," he said to himself. He put one foot in. Then the other. Ever so slowly, he waded up to his ankles. His brow furrowed. Was he scared of the water? He waded up to his knees. Then up to his waist. "You can do this," he said again. Meeshell didn't really know Humphrey, but she wanted to encourage him. *Go ahead*, she thought. *It'll be okay. The water will hold you up. Well, at least it does for mermaids.*

As if hearing her thoughts, he tossed the floaties onto the shore. And that's when everything went royally wrong.

Humphrey disappeared under the water.

Little bubbles appeared at the surface, but Humphrey didn't come back up. Meeshell waited. How long could a land-dweller hold his breath? She wasn't quite sure. Even the cranes watched nervously. And then the bubbles stopped.

Uh-oh.

Meeshell dived, swimming as fast as she could. She found him, struggling at the bottom of the lake. His back was to her, so she put her arms around his waist and pulled him to the surface. He took a huge gasp of air. Once she was certain he was breathing, she gave a strong push with her tail, sending him onto the shore. Then she swam into the depths

so he wouldn't be able to see her tail. "You okay?" she asked.

He sat up and coughed a few times. Then he wiped his mouth with the back of his hand. "Yeah, I'm okay." He looked at her. "You...you saved me. Thank you."

"You're welcome." She swam a bit deeper, worried the full moon would give her away.

Humphrey coughed again. "I didn't know anyone was here. I...I thought I was alone." He was still struggling a bit to catch his breath.

"Maybe you should take some swim lessons," she said. She was trying to be helpful, but he looked insulted.

"Swim lessons?" He scrambled to his feet. Water dripped down his legs. "I don't need lessons. I can swim. I'm not afraid of water. What gave you that idea? I...I swim all the time."

"Uh, okay, I didn't mean to—"

"I came here to get some exercise, because I'm *not* afraid of the water. And because I *can* swim. But

then I got a cramp. In my leg. That's why I sank to the bottom."

He wasn't going to admit that he couldn't swim. As if he was ashamed of that fact. She wanted to tell him it was no big deal, that everyone has something they can't do, and that she of all people knew how embarrassing it was to have people think you're afraid of something most other people aren't afraid of…but she felt too shy to tell him something so personal. Plus, she knew he was trying to teach himself, and she'd been a witness to something he'd wanted to keep secret.

A chime sounded. Humphrey looked at his watch. "Curfew. We'd better go."

She couldn't get out of the water and let him see her tail. "Um, could you turn around? I need to change."

"Of course," he said, turning his back. She pulled herself out, grabbed the towel, and dried quickly. Her legs returned and she slipped her coat back on. Then together, they hurried down the path. He

didn't say anything else, nor did she. But as he headed toward the boys' dormitory, with his floaties in hand, she realized something.

She'd saved a prince from drowning, just like her mother before her. Did this mean that Humphrey was her destined prince? No way. She and Humphrey seemed to have nothing in common. Except for the fact that they were both shy. And everyone knows that two extremely shy people could *never* work together.

Could they?

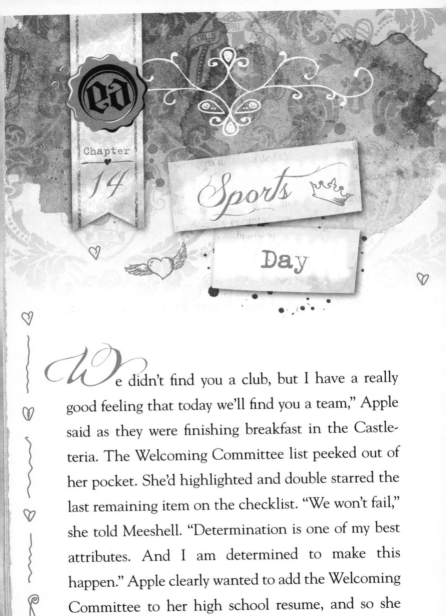

Chapter 14

Sports Day

We didn't find you a club, but I have a really good feeling that today we'll find you a team," Apple said as they were finishing breakfast in the Castleteria. The Welcoming Committee list peeked out of her pocket. She'd highlighted and double starred the last remaining item on the checklist. "We won't fail," she told Meeshell. "Determination is one of my best attributes. And I am determined to make this happen." Apple clearly wanted to add the Welcoming Committee to her high school resume, and so she needed Meeshell to join something. Meeshell also wanted to find something—she really wanted to have a full experience at Ever After High, like her father had—but Apple's list was adding pressure to the situation. Meeshell didn't want to disappoint anyone, especially Apple, who'd been so nice to her.

Sports Day was similar to Club Day, except that it was set up on the athletic field. All the teams were represented, with athletes present to answer questions, and coaches ready to hold tryouts.

"Ashlynn mentioned cheerhexing. Would you like to give that a try?"

At that moment, a pair of fairies flew past, the gust from their wings nearly knocking Meeshell over. The fairies laughed wickedly. They wore matching shimmering skirts, T-shirts with the letters *EAH*, and carried red pom-poms. They landed next to other students who were dressed in the same outfits. Ashlynn was among them. She called out Meeshell's name and waved.

"I...I guess I'll give it a try," Meeshell said.

But as they approached the squad, Meeshell realized she was about to make a huge mistake. The cheerhexing squad was no longer standing still. They'd erupted into a frenzy of movement, flinging themselves around, leaping, twirling, flipping, then landing on their feet with precision. Meeshell had leaped out of the water many times, and she'd done her fair share of flips, but those moves had been propelled by the power of her tail. She didn't know how to use her legs to do such things.

Then the squad performed a cheer.

> "Spell!
> Say what? Say what?
> Spell!
> That's what we do!
> We spell,
> We spell for you!"

Meeshell cringed. Those moves were way too complicated!

"What do you think?" Ashlynn asked Meeshell when the cheer was over. "You think you want to join? It's really fun."

"Uh…" There was no chance to opt out because a tall, scowling fairy was flying straight toward Meeshell. A thick turquoise streak ran through the fairy's shimmering blond hair. Her wings were iridescent and caught the sun's rays like a prism.

Ashlynn looked nervously at the fairy, then hurried back to the squad. "Good luck!" she called to Meeshell over her shoulder.

The fairy hovered in front of Meeshell. "Don't tell me *you're* going to try out," the fairy said in a snippy way. Meeshell recognized her. This was the same fairy who had made fun of her dress on the first day.

Faybelle didn't wait for Meeshell to answer. Instead she turned to Apple. "Why are *you* here?"

"I'm here because I've been assigned to help Meeshell. I'm her Welcoming Committee representative." Apple leaned close to Faybelle and frowned.

"Be nice to her, Faybelle. She's new and that means she's not used to your…*wickedness*."

Faybelle's mouth turned up, ever so slightly, and ever so wickedly. "Oh, I'll *be nice* to her."

"Good. I appreciate that." Apple beamed. Hadn't she heard the sarcasm in Faybelle's voice? Apple patted Meeshell's shoulder. "I'll wait over there while you try out." Then she grabbed Meeshell's bag and MirrorPad, and sat on a nearby bench.

Faybelle, still hovering, crossed her arms and gave Meeshell a very long, very intense look. "So?" she asked. "What can you do? Front flips? Backflips? Somersaults? Cartwheels? Handstands?"

At this point in time, Meeshell was grateful that she could *stand* without falling over. But obviously that wouldn't be enough.

"I'm not sure what I can do," she answered. "I've never been a cheerhexer before."

Faybelle rolled her eyes. "Oh, that's just spelltacular news." Her wings folded and she landed on the soft grass. Then she did a forward roll and sprang back to her feet. She pushed a strand of hair from her forehead. "Let me see you do that."

Apple gave Meeshell two enthusiastic thumbs-up. Ashlynn beamed an encouraging smile.

That didn't look so difficult, Meeshell thought. In fact, it reminded her of the kind of roll she did all the time when she was swimming and wanted to change directions. She decided that she might as well give it a try. How else would she know what she was capable of if she didn't try? So, with a deep steadying breath, she stepped onto the field and attempted a forward roll.

Graceful was not a word to describe what happened next. Nor was *skillful* or *coordinated*. Meeshell wasn't sure how she ended up sideways. She'd closed her eyes, she'd leaned forward with the intent to roll, but somehow she went wonky.

"How embarrassing for you," Faybelle said with a snort once Meeshell sat up. Then Faybelle rose into the air again, her wings beating with annoyance. "Newsflash, new girl, I don't have time to train amateurs." Then she flew over to another hopeful candidate.

"Okay, so cheerhexing's not your thing," Apple said as Meeshell picked blades of grass out of her hair. "It's not for everyone—mostly just for fairies, in fact! But there are many more tryouts going on. Follow me." With a tug on Meeshell's hand, Apple exuberantly pulled her down the field, her determination steadfast. As much as Meeshell liked Apple, she wished she could make that Welcoming Committee list disappear. Maybe Farrah could grant that wish for her?

Apple led Meeshell right up to an odd little man. His neck, arms, and legs were equally thick and blocky. His shirt was tucked into his gym shorts and he wore a pair of kneesocks with his tennis shoes. A whistle hung around his neck. While he looked kinda funny, he smelled *delicious*, like something

that had been baked in an oven. "Coach Ginger-breadman, this is Meeshell, our newest student. Can she try out for the team?"

"You want to try out for Track and Shield?" Coach Gingerbreadman asked. "What are you interested in doing?"

Meeshell remembered that her father had been on the Track and Shield team when he went to Ever After High. "What choices do I have?" she asked.

"Well, we've already got a long-jump champion." He pointed to a boy who was jumping across a sand-pit. It was the same prince she'd seen earlier, the one who'd turned into a frog. Wow, could he jump! "And we've got plenty of students for the shield toss." He pointed to a bunch of students who were flinging shields at a target. "But you know, I could use some more sprinters. Can you run, run, run as fast as you can?"

Both Apple and Coach Gingerbreadman looked expectantly at Meeshell, who gulped. She hadn't yet tried to run, let alone as fast as she could. How did that work, exactly? "I have a good feeling about this," Apple said. "I'll just sit over here." Once again, she sat on a nearby bench.

"Start on this line," Coach Gingerbreadman said. "And run to that line." He pointed down the track. "I'll time you." Waddling on his thick legs, he made his way to the finish line. Then he turned and hollered at her. "Take your mark!"

She stood on the start line.

"Get set!"

What was she supposed to do? She looked down at her legs.

"Run, run, run!" He blew his whistle.

Fast was not a word to describe what happened next. Nor was *swift* or *speedy*. She told her legs to move. And they did. But her knees came up real high at first, as if she were a prancing horse. Then, once she'd gotten the knees to settle down, she couldn't keep a straight line. She'd veered to the left, then to the right. By the time she'd reached the

finish line, completely out of breath, Coach Ginger-breadman was standing with his mouth hanging open, aghast at what he'd just witnessed.

"What was that?" he asked.

"That was…" She took a huge breath. "That was running."

"Not in my playbook!" He shook his head. "If I didn't know better, I'd guess you'd never used your legs before."

Meeshell didn't disagree with him.

Apple was beginning to look a little desperate. "You want to keep trying? What about Grimmnastics? Oh no, that won't work since you'd probably have to do somersaults. What about Sorcerer's Soccer? Oh drat, that requires running. What about swim team? Oops, that won't work either, since you're afraid of water." She frowned. "I'm not sure what to do."

"It's okay," Meeshell said. She could tell how disappointed Apple was, and she felt badly. Especially knowing she'd be a perfect fit for the swim team…

if only she could tell Apple the truth about who she really was.

While other students walked past, wearing their new uniforms and carrying banners for their new teams, Meeshell had nothing.

The Secret

Prince

When Meeshell got back to her dorm room after dinner, she collapsed onto her bed. Thankfully, Farrah wasn't there, so Meeshell didn't have to put on a brave face. The day had been an epic fail! She felt as if she'd been thrown for a loop. Even the ever-cheerful Apple had seemed discouraged.

Maybe Meeshell wouldn't join a club or a team. She didn't need a bunch of new friends. She didn't need to be popular. But from what Apple had said, being in a club was part of the Ever After High experience, and experiencing normal life on land was Meeshell's goal.

She checked her messages. The first was from Professor Baba Yaga, reminding her to check in if anything was wrong. The second message was from Hagatha, alerting students that there would be no green bean hash next week, due to a union dispute with the giants. And the third message was from Mrs. Her Majesty the White Queen with the throne-work assignment for Princessology.

MirrorPad in hand, Meeshell sat on the balcony, her legs curled beneath her. Where was a seagull when she needed one? She really wanted to send a message home. She really wanted to talk to her Merfriends. To someone who'd understand.

StoryTeller2: Hi. How are you doing?

The MirrorPad lit up, startling Meeshell. It was as if StoryTeller2 could read her mind, knowing she needed someone to talk to!

Seashell: Not so good.

StoryTeller2: How come?

Seashell: I tried out for cheerhexing and Track and Shield today, and I was a total disaster.

StoryTeller2: Yeah, I heard.

Seashell: You heard?

StoryTeller2: Word gets around. Blondie Lockes showed some highlights on her *Just Right* show. You can't keep any secrets at Ever After High.

She sure hoped that last statement wasn't true.

StoryTeller2: Don't feel too bad. I'm not good at sports, either. Why are athletes always popular? I don't get it. When will intelligence and artistic creativity get as much attention as sports?

Seashell: Thanks for trying to make me feel better. But it was hextremely embarrassing.

StoryTeller2: Believe me, I know embarrassing. And what I saw wasn't all that bad. At
least you didn't fall flat on your face. I do that
all the time.

Seashell: You do?

StoryTeller2: Yep. A bit of a klutz.

She felt better knowing that she wasn't the only
klutz on campus.

Seashell: So, you obviously know who I am
but I don't know who you are. Who are you?

As usual, a long pause followed.

Seashell: Hello?

Another long pause with no response.

Seashell: You still there?

Whoever was conversing with Meeshell clearly didn't want to reveal his or her true identity. But why? It seemed strange to her. Yet how could she feel annoyed, when she was also hiding her true identity?

> **Seashell**: Okay, you don't have to tell me who you are. But can you tell me just one thing about yourself? Just a little hint?
> **StoryTeller2**: Just one thing?
> **Seashell**: Yes. One thing and I'll stop asking.
> **StoryTeller2**: I'm a prince.

A prince? Her heart flitted for a moment. Not only did this mysterious person seem nice *and* sensitive, but he was also a prince? She'd promised to ask only one thing, but now a stream of questions flooded her mind. And one question in particular lingered.

Are you my prince?

The next morning Apple was back to her usual cheerful self. "We're going to Mirror Beach," she said. "Will you join us?"

"But Meeshell's afraid of the water," Ashlynn reminded her. The girls were dressed in bathing suits, with bright cover-ups and flip-flops.

"Oh hex, that's right." Apple carried a large beach bag stuffed with towels, swimming goggles, and sunscreen. "If you sit in the sand, and don't go near the water, will you come with us?"

Meeshell glanced at the thronework waiting on her desk. Yes, it needed to get done, but hanging out on the beach would be lovely. She missed the salty spray. The sound of gulls. The rhythm of the waves. As long as she stayed away from the water and kept her legs perfectly dry, she'd be fine. "I'd love to come with you."

"Spelltacular!"

Mirror Beach was a short walk from the dock where the *Narwhal* had delivered Meeshell. The sand was white, with tiny ground-up seashells that made it sparkle. A tall wooden chair had been built in the center of the beach. Perched at the top was a boy she hadn't yet met. He wore sunglasses and striped swim trunks. A sign hanging on the back of the chair read:

LIFEGUARD ON DUTY

When he saw them approaching, he waved. The girls waved back. "That's Ashlynn's boyfriend," Apple explained. "His name is Hunter."

Hunter scrambled down from the chair and planted a big smooch on Ashlynn's cheek. "Hi, Apple. Hi, Meeshell. It's great to finally meet you. Welcome to Mirror Beach."

"Thanks." Meeshell took a deep breath, the salt air filling her lungs. It felt so good to be near the sea! She couldn't take her eyes off the water. It was calling to her, as if it had a voice. She felt twitchy again. Her legs began to ache, wanting to be turned into a tail.

The girls quickly set up a large umbrella and some beach chairs as Hunter returned to his station. Ashlynn had packed snacks in a basket. She passed them each a bottle of Ice Queen Glacier Water. Meeshell settled into a chair. Apple handed out the sunblock, explaining its importance in keeping her the "fairest in the land." Then they nibbled on mini throne-cakes. The crumbs attracted a pair of gulls. Meeshell smiled at them. This was her chance to get a message home!

While Apple and Ashlynn busily applied some

sunblock, Meeshell leaned close to one of the gulls and spoke in his language. "Can you get a message to the king and queen of the Merpeople" The gull nodded. The gull, of course, knew Meeshell's true identity, for all creatures of the sea know a mermaid when they see one. "Please tell them that I am fine and that I miss them." The gull nodded again. She rewarded him with a corner of thronecake. He ate it, then flew off to deliver the message.

"I don't mean to pry, but were you speaking Gull to that seagull?" Ashlynn asked, her eyes lighting up. "I thought I was the only one who could talk to birds. Where did you learn?"

Meeshell hesitated for a moment. She didn't want to tell another lie. But Ashlynn had clearly caught her speaking Gull. "We have to take many languages at school in my kingdom," she explained. "I learned Gull at school. I know quite a few animal languages, actually."

Ashlynn's face lit up. "Oh, me too, I know all sorts. Maybe we can tutor each other. I don't know

a word of Gull, but I know Owl really well. And Phoenix."

Meeshell was relieved that Ashlynn hadn't understood her conversation with the gull. But learning new languages sounded like a lovely idea, and she was about to say so when a voice nearby hollered, "Catch a wave!"

A bunch of students, each carrying a surfboard, ran past. Daring Charming was in the lead, his family crest plastered across his swim trunks. He turned and smiled, and this time Meeshell remembered to close her eyes until the brilliance had faded. Apple waved to him, as did Ashlynn. Following behind the pack was Humphrey. He stumbled under the weight of his surfboard, then plunked it into the water. He wasn't wearing his arm floaties this time, which seemed a bit dangerous to Meeshell since she suspected he couldn't swim. Daring and his crew headed straight into the water, then paddled out toward a wave as it began to crest. She'd seen land-dwellers surf before. But back home, she and

her Merfriends didn't need special equipment to surf. Their tails were better than boards. And surfing was always good because Meeshell and her Merfriends all had the magical ability to make water ebb and flow at their will.

Meeshell watched with envy as Daring jumped onto his board, riding the wave with ease and grace. As his hair billowed, a few of his groupies stood on shore taking photos of him.

"That's another club," Apple explained. "The Surf Club. But with your fear of water, obviously not a good choice."

"You're right," Meeshell said. "It's not for me."

Humphrey hadn't caught the wave. He sat on his board, floating close to shore. Unlike the others, he was frowning and nervously looking around.

"I…I'm just going to stretch my legs," Meeshell told the other two. Then she walked slowly down the beach toward Humphrey. But as she walked and tried to ignore the urge to throw herself into the water, she overheard Apple confiding in Ashlynn.

"I'm disappointed in myself," Apple said. "I had a simple assignment for the Welcoming Committee and I've failed."

"It's not your fault that Meeshell's having trouble fitting in," Ashlynn said kindly.

"It *is* my fault. There's a place for everybody. I just have to think harder." Apple paused to think. "It's odd. I'm usually such a good judge of character. But for some reason, I can't figure Meeshell out. I'm not sure why."

Meeshell hated that Apple felt so much pressure to help her. It would be so easy to find a club or team if she stopped pretending to be someone she wasn't. But that would interfere with her plan.

Meeshell walked closer to the water's edge. She passed Daring's groupies. "Poor Daring," one of them said. "Where did the waves go?"

True enough, Daring and his fellow Surf Club members sat on their boards, floating, with no waves in sight. The sea had suddenly turned calm and now all the surfers were wearing frowns.

"Humphrey," Meeshell called. Her voice startled him so much, he almost fell off his board.

"Uh…uh…h-hi," he stammered.

She stood at the water's edge, making sure her feet didn't touch the water. "You don't have your floaties."

"Huh?" His face turned bright red and he laughed in a nervous way. "I don't know what you're talking about. I don't need floaties. I love surfing. I surf all the time." And with that, he leaned forward and began paddling with his arms until he reached Daring and the others in the deeper water.

Well, maybe she'd been wrong. Maybe he had gotten a leg cramp at the lake, and maybe he was a good swimmer after all. There was no reason for him to lie to her.

"Where are the waves?" one of the surfers shouted.

"Waves, waves, waves!" they all began to chant, even Humphrey.

They clearly wanted to surf. And she could help. Coral's spell had transformed Meeshell's tail into

two legs, but it hadn't transformed her magic touch. She'd been able to conjure that little wave that had pushed the *Narwhal* across the ocean. Could she risk using magic now to help create waves for the surfers?

She glanced over her shoulder. Apple and Ashlynn had walked to the Snack Shack to order shaved ice. Their backs were turned to her. Careful to keep her feet dry, she quickly reached out and touched the water. That's all it took. Her hand retreated quickly. No one noticed.

The wave came right away. The surfers cheered. Meeshell smiled proudly. She stepped backward, moving up the beach to avoid the wave, but keeping her eyes focused on the surfers. She didn't want to miss a moment of the hexcitment as they rode the magic wave. But something was wrong. The wave grew bigger and bigger. Oh no, what had she done? The surfers shrieked and paddled toward shore as fast as they could. Then they leaped from the water as the wave reached for the sky, roiling and foaming.

The lifeguard whistle blew. "Run!" Hunter cried. Meeshell ran, along with everyone else until they'd made it safely up the path. Then they turned and watched with horror as the wave crashed onto the beach, splitting the lifeguard chair in two. Luckily, Hunter had leaped away in time.

"Where's Humphrey?" Daring asked.

Meeshell looked around. Humphrey had disappeared!

anic welled in Meeshell's chest. She frantically looked around. Apple, Ashlynn, and Hunter were standing next to her. The students who ran the Snack Shack were also there, along with a group who'd been playing beach volleyball. Daring and the members of the Surf Club were also safe. It appeared that everyone had avoided the rogue wave.

Except for one person.

"There he is!" Meeshell cried, pointing down the

beach where a shape lay in the sand. A mangled surfboard lay a few feet away.

What had she done? She had no idea how she got her legs to move as quickly as they did, but she flew down the beach and threw herself next to him. He lay on his back, his arms and legs splayed, his eyes closed. A crab skittered across his chest. While the others ran to catch up, she put her ear to Humphrey's chest. "He's breathing," she announced as Hunter and Daring knelt beside her. She almost burst into tears of relief.

"He's stunned," Hunter said. He and Daring helped Humphrey sit upright. Humphrey took a huge breath, then opened his eyes. "You okay?" Hunter asked.

After a few minutes of coughing, Humphrey reached up and felt his head. "No cracks. I'm okay. But that wave really tossed me around. I thought I was going to be crushed." He picked a piece of seaweed off his face.

"Sounds like the time in Hero Training when I got caught in the middle of a griffin stampede," Daring said. "But we survived. Good job, Dumpty." Then he slapped Humphrey on the back, bringing about another coughing fit. A pair of nurse fairies appeared. They flitted around Humphrey's head, then gave two thumbs-up and flew away.

Hunter helped Humphrey to his feet. All the other students had gathered 'round. Humphrey glanced at Meeshell, looking more embarrassed than ever.

"I'm sorry," she told him.

"Why are you sorry?" Hunter asked. "You were the first to reach him. You practically saved him." Hunter was congratulating her? That wasn't fair. She'd almost squashed Humphrey with the giant wave she'd created! "You've got good eyes. Would you like to join the lifeguard crew?"

"But Meeshell's afraid of water," Ashlynn said before Meeshell could reply.

"Afraid of the water?" Hunter asked. "That's too bad. We really need more help."

It was definitely too bad, because of all the students at Ever After High, Meeshell knew she'd be a superb lifeguard. She'd be able to conduct rescues underwater, and reach swimming speeds that no land-dweller could reach. If she admitted, right then and there, the truth about being a mermaid, then she could help Hunter save lives!

If she spoke up and told everyone she was a mermaid, and explained that she wasn't really afraid of water, her new friends would see that she was brave and fun-loving, just like they were. All of the things that must have seemed so odd about her, that they had been so kind and accepting of, would suddenly make sense. Sure, she was a little shy, but she wasn't yet used to life on land.

But admitting she was a mermaid would mean being treated differently. And that would mean losing a chance at having the authentic experience as a land-dweller. But the urge to tell the truth was overwhelming.

"I...I need to go," she blurted. As Meeshell hurried away, Hunter blew on his whistle.

"Okay, everyone," he called. "The rogue wave is gone. You can go back into the water!"

---

*O*nce again, when she got back to the dormitory, Meeshell collapsed onto her bed. What a total disaster the week had been. Trying to be a land-dweller was really hard. She hadn't found a club, she'd failed at two team tryouts, and now she'd almost drowned everyone! She reached out to the one person who seemed to understand her.

> **Seashell**: I feel like a total loser.
>
> **StoryTeller2**: How come?
>
> **Seashell**: Every time I try to do something, it doesn't work.

StoryTeller2: Yeah, been there, done that. I feel that way a lot.

Seashell: Do you ever wish you were someone else?

StoryTeller2: All the time.

Seashell: Really? Why?

StoryTeller2: Because I don't fit in. I never know what to say.

Seashell: I never knew what it felt like to not fit in, but now I do.

StoryTeller2: Like a fish out of water.

Seashell: You have no idea how true that is.

She really wanted to meet her mysterious friend—this prince who wanted to hide his identity. Then it occurred to her that maybe he wasn't a prince after all. He could be a troll for all she knew. It didn't matter either way because she didn't care about his royal status. Or two-footed status. She felt as if she could tell him anything. And that he'd understand and be sympathetic.

Seashell: Will you please tell me who you are?

StoryTeller2: Believe me, you won't be impressed.

Seashell: Why do I need to be impressed? You're my friend.

Long pause.

StoryTeller2: I gotta go do something. Bye.

She'd scared him off again.

"Meeshell, can we talk?" Apple had poked her head into the room. Her voice was more serious than usual.

"Sure," Meeshell said. She set aside the Mirror-Pad, then pushed a pile of pillows off the bed so Apple could sit next to her.

"As you ran from the beach, I realized something." Apple took the Welcoming Committee list from her pocket. "When I offered to be your Welcoming

Committee representative, I wasn't thinking about you. I was thinking about myself."

"That's not true."

"Yes, it is. It's always been very important to me that I do things right, you know? That I meet my goals and succeed. I really wanted to be a part of this committee with Briar because she's one of my best friends forever after, and because it would look good on my records. But the truth is, it doesn't matter if I'm on another committee. What matters is that you're happy. And I think I've been putting too much pressure on you. You don't have to join a club or be on a team to fit in here at Ever After High. You don't have to belong to anything if you don't want to. That's perfectly okay." She crumpled the list in her hand, then tossed it into the recycling bin. "So from this moment on, I'm going to stop putting pressure on you. You do what makes you happy, Meeshell." She gave her a hug. "And I hope we can be BFFAs."

Meeshell smiled gratefully at Apple. She really was one of the sweetest people Meeshell had ever met. "Of course. Thank you, Apple."

After Apple left, Meeshell walked onto the balcony and gazed out over the school grounds. Ashlynn and a few other cheerhexers, dressed in their uniforms, were walking together across the quad. Some Track and Shield runners were sitting at the edge of the track, laughing about something. A couple of guys from the Tech Club were at a table, trying to untangle a huge pile of cords. At that moment, Meeshell felt very alone. Apple had said that Meeshell didn't need to join a club or team to fit in. But finding other students who shared the same interests or talents would definitely help.

A figure floated in front of her. Meeshell gasped. "Oh, Professor Yaga, you startled me."

The elderly woman sat crossed-legged on her pillow, hovering in front of the balcony. "I need your assistance," she explained. "Come with me."

Meeshell had to walk quickly to keep up with Professor Yaga's floating pillow. The professor led her away from the main campus, down a path, to a modern building built on a bluff above the sea.

"We have an extensive Beastology program of study here at Ever After High. There is a stable for the hoofed creatures, an aviary for the winged beasts. But this is the Creature Care Center, where injured or sick creatures are treated." Professor Yaga opened

the door and ushered Meeshell into the building. "They receive the best possible care, of course, and we in turn learn a lot from them. And this room is where we treat creatures of the sea."

Meeshell squealed with delight. She stood facing an aquarium so vast that it spanned the length of the building and reached all the way to the ceiling. She pressed her face against the glass. Inside, eels peered out from rocky burrows, sea horses stampeded across bright coral, peacock fish fanned their tails. A thick kelp forest grew on one side of the tank. It reminded her of home. "This is a class?" Meeshell asked.

"Beast Care and Magicment is a specialty class," the professor confirmed. "Most of these creatures are here to enrich the curriculum. When their injuries or illnesses heal, they will be released back into the wild. But a few are pets." She pointed to a strange little fish in the corner that looked to be made out of candy. "Ginger Breadhouse insists on bringing her gummy fish here for playdates." The fish waved at Meeshell. Meeshell waved back.

Professor Yaga got off her pillow, then led Meeshell to a section of the aquarium where a small cave was set in a coral reef. "Yesterday, one of the students found an octopus on the beach," she told Meeshell. "The creature appeared disoriented and had suffered some trauma. We set her into this tank, and we were going to conduct our examination today, but she seems to have disappeared."

"You think she escaped?" Meeshell asked. She noticed that the aquarium didn't have a cover, so it was open.

"That is doubtful. I placed a magical spell on this aquarium that doesn't allow the injured creatures to escape. We want to keep them here, at least until they are well again." The professor peered through the glass. "No one has seen her since last night."

Meeshell looked carefully. She had an idea as to what was going on. "She is probably using her powers of camouflage to avoid us. Octopuses are very shy creatures. I can try to go in and communicate with her, to let her know we only want to help her, but I can't guarantee success."

"I understand. But we must try. If she doesn't get help, she might perish."

Professor Yaga and Meeshell pushed a stepladder across the floor, then rested it against the tank. Meeshell climbed the steps until she reached the top of the aquarium. She looked down at the professor. "We're alone, right? No one will see me?"

"Correct."

Meeshell climbed into the tank. Just as she began to tread water, her legs twitched, then turned into a tail. She swam directly to the cave, then stuck her head into its opening. It was empty. She swam around the tank, her eyes peeled for signs of tentacles, but Meeshell knew that if the octopus wanted to stay hidden, no one would be able to find her. So, once she reached the center of the tank, she began to speak in the language of all cephalopods. Using the tip of her tail, she tapped against a rock. It was a complicated language, but one she'd recently mastered. *Do not worry*, she tapped. *These land-dwellers are not going to eat you. They want to help you.*

The octopus did not appear. Was it possible that she had escaped, despite the magic spell? It wouldn't surprise Meeshell, for octopuses were among the most intelligent creatures in the sea.

She swam to another section, where the coral reef ended and the kelp reef began. The feel of the kelp against her skin was lovely. Homesickness washed over her. She found another rock and began tapping again. *The land-dwellers want to help you. You've been hurt and they can help make you better. Please come out of hiding.* She waited, her gaze still searching, looking for any shape that seemed unusual.

A tapping sound followed. *Do you promise they won't eat me?*

She tapped back. *Yes, I promise.*

What had looked like a gray rock, resting in the sand, slowly turned orange. The octopus stretched

out her seven tentacles. The eighth, however, she held close. It appeared to have suffered a gash.

Meeshell swam up to the octopus. She was larger than most, which meant she was advanced in years. Meeshell tapped again. *How are you feeling?*

My tentacle got caught in a net. It is damaged.

Meeshell gently reached out and examined the injured tentacle. The gash was deep. She looked over at the glass, where Professor Yaga stood. The professor pointed upward, to an examination station that was built at the top of the aquarium.

We must go to the surface so your injury can be treated. Do you need my help? Meeshell tapped.

Yes.

Meeshell stretched out her tail. The octopus climbed on and held tightly as Meeshell slowly swam to the surface. Professor Yaga, thanks to her unique mode of pillow travel, met them and helped transfer the octopus onto a smooth platform. The creature quivered. Meeshell held one of her uninjured tentacles. *Do not be afraid*, she tapped. *This land-dweller will help you.*

Meeshell watched while the professor mixed a potion and applied it to the injury. "Is that magic?" Meeshell asked.

"It is not magic," the professor explained. "It is an ointment that will help keep the infection from spreading."

"Does it contain powdered urchin shell?"

Professor Yaga raised her gray eyebrows. "No, it doesn't."

Meeshell wasn't trying to tell the professor what to do, but she thought she should share this important information. "In the Merkingdom, we use powdered urchin shells to thicken our ointments so they will better adhere to the wound."

"That is most ingenious." The professor floated to a cabinet, searched around until she found a small vial, then brought the vial back to the examination platform. "Perhaps you would like to instruct me?"

Meeshell mixed the powder into the ointment, then applied it to the wound. Then she took a clear, waterproof bandage and wrapped the tentacle. The octopus held perfectly still, watching with her big, watery eyes. *Does it hurt?* Meeshell tapped.

No, the octopus replied. *It feels much better!*

Then Meeshell eased the creature back into the water. "Please tell her that she will need to stay here for a few more days to recover," Professor Yaga said.

Meeshell told the octopus. The creature thanked her, then glided back to the cave.

Meeshell took one more swim, then sat on the platform. Professor Yaga mumbled a magic spell and Meeshell's tail and clothing instantly dried. Two-footed once again, she climbed down the ladder. She looked back into the aquarium. The octopus peeked out of her cave and waved.

As they left the aquarium, Professor Yaga floating on her pillow, Meeshell walking alongside, the professor asked Meeshell how she was doing. Meeshell took a long breath. "Not very well," she admitted.

"Everyone has been really nice to me, but...but I'm not sure what to do with myself. I mean, everyone seems to have found a place where they belong. But I haven't found that yet. I don't know what else to do."

Professor Yaga pressed her fingertips together. "Perhaps the best way to solve your dilemma is to think about the octopus."

"How so?"

"Camouflage helps the octopus hide and survive predators. But when she takes on the color of a rock, she doesn't pretend to be a rock. When she takes on the color of an electric eel, she doesn't pretend to be an eel. She is always herself. Do you see what I'm getting at?" Meeshell shook her head. The professor spun around on her pillow so she was facing Meeshell. "You are having trouble fitting in because you are trying to be what you are not."

"But if I pretend to be a land-dweller, then people will treat me like one. And then I'll have a *real*, land-dwelling experience."

The professor smiled knowingly. "The only *real* experience, my dear, is the experience in which you are your *real* self." Then she turned back around.

As Meeshell and the professor made their way back to campus, Meeshell realized that she had a lot to think about.

The True

Tale

*A*fter leaving the professor, Meeshell stood in the center of the quad. The other students were inside the Castleteria, eating dinner. The sky had not yet darkened, so the twinkling above her head was not from stars but from a procession of cleaning fairies who were leaving the school grounds, heading to their forest homes. As Meeshell wiped specks of fairy dust from her face, she thought about the professor's words.

The only real *experience is the experience in which you are your* real *self.*

Was that true?

She felt fidgety again. She couldn't think clearly. Was her confusion a side effect of all the air she'd been exposed to? Even though she'd just had a lovely swim in the aquarium, she wanted more time in the water. Time to be herself and think.

She ran down the narrow path, all the way to the lake. When she got there, she jumped straight in. The golden cranes made room for her as she swam. As her tail beat a rhythm, her doubts washed away. She stopped worrying about wanting to fit in. She felt great—so great that she stuck her head above the surface and sang. How good it felt to sing! How she'd missed it. Then, when she reached a high note, she leaped out of the water.

And that's when she noticed Apple, Maddie, Ashlynn, and Briar all standing on the bank, watching her with mouths wide open. The girls were

stunned silent. For a long, tense moment, Meeshell waited to hear what her friends would say.

"Meeshell! You're a mermaid!" Ashlynn blurted out. The girls laughed, and just like that, all the tension was gone.

"Yes, I am a mermaid. So I'm not really afraid of water. I'm so sorry I lied to you. My legs turn back into my tail when I touch water. That's why I acted so strangely."

"I knew it," Maddie said. "How could anybody not like my hat?"

"Why were you pretending to be someone else?" Briar asked.

"Because…" Meeshell looked down at her tail. "I'm just not very confident around people when I'm on land. I'd never really been around people before coming to Ever After High."

"I think you're doing a wonderlandiful job of being around people on land," Maddie replied. Meeshell smiled appreciatively.

"You all have made it so easy for me. But I also hid who I was because my future is living on land, without my tail, and without my singing voice. I wanted to see what that would be like. To see if I could make it work."

Apple sat next to her, a look of absolute understanding on her face. "Meeshell, we each have futures waiting for us. But what I've learned is this— that we can't control them. Yes, there are things that we're supposed to do. Things that are expected and foretold. When I first got to Ever After High, I tried to live for my future life. I tried to convince Raven that she had to be someone other than who she really is, just to fit this future life. But what I've figured out is that we can't live for the future. We have to be our true selves right now. In this moment."

Briar, Maddie, and Ashlynn all nodded. The little mouse peeked out of Maddie's hat, and he nodded, too.

Then Apple put an arm around Meeshell. "The Little Mermaid is my favorite fairytale ever after.

Now it makes sense. I couldn't help you find a club because I didn't know the *real* you. You would be a spelltacular fit for the Happily-Glees!" She stopped smiling and withdrew her arm. "But of course, only if *you* want."

Meeshell laughed. "Yes, I'd really like to join the Happily-Glees! I've wanted to join since I first saw them in the quad."

"Since you're a mermaid, I think you should also join Hunter's lifeguard squad," Ashlynn said. "You'd be the best lifeguard Ever After High has ever seen!"

"And what about the swim team?" Briar asked. "A mermaid would set some records for sure."

"I think you should join the Teapot Club," Maddie said. They all looked at her quizzically.

"I don't get it," Briar said. "What do mermaids and teapots have in common?"

"Oh, a riddle!" Maddie said, clapping her hands. "I don't know. What *do* mermaids and teapots have in common?"

Briar peered over her crownglasses. "Uh, I was asking you."

"Well, how am I supposed to know the answer? It's not *my* riddle, you silly." Then Maddie took a crumpet from her teapot hat and began feeding the golden cranes.

Meeshell couldn't believe how relieved she felt. Yes, they all knew she was a mermaid. Yes, they were treating her differently. But that was okay. Because right now, this was who she was—a Mergirl going to Ever After High. She hadn't yet given up her voice. She hadn't yet given up her tail. That was in the future. And when that time came, she'd be that girl. She couldn't live trying to be her future self. That didn't make sense. In the end it didn't matter what anyone thought of her, it only mattered what she thought of herself. She had to be her true self to be happy.

Just as Meeshell's tail dried and her legs reappeared, a nearby mirror lit up. Blondie Lockes's

face appeared. "Listen up, my fellow fairytales, have I got a very hexciting scoop for you. It turns out that our newest student, Meeshell, is actually a mermaid!"

Wow, that girl was good.

The Happily-Glees

*M*eeshell and her fellow Happily-Glees stood in the wing of the Charmitorium's stage, waiting to be announced. The air around them sizzled with nervous energy and excitement. It was the night of the annual Ever After High Talent Show. The Happily-Glees were one of dozens of acts scheduled to perform in front of the entire student body. Duchess Swan and her pet swan, Pirouette, were waiting to dance a *pas de deux* in matching tutus. Ginger Breadhouse had prepared a magic trick with singing sprinkles and flying moonpies. And Sparrow Hood and the Merry Men were currently on stage, playing the school's anthem to warm up the crowd.

Meeshell went over her lyrics in her head. The choir had practiced all weekend. Meeshell had learned the solo part, while the rest of the choir had learned the harmony. With Meeshell's voice taking the lead, the other singers grew more confident, and the whole choir began to sound better. Melody decided to cut back on the choreography, instead focusing entirely on the music. The transition in her choir was amazing. "I'm so proud of each of you," she whispered as they huddled together. "Let's go out there and give them a performance they'll never forget." Then she paused, probably remembering the last performance, which had yet to be forgotten. "I meant that in a *good* way." They all chuckled.

Meeshell peeked past the stage's curtain. There were no empty seats in the Charmitorium. Even the balcony was full. Tech Club members busily worked the lights, the sound system, and cameras. Humphrey stood behind one of the cameras. He glanced at Meeshell. She waved at him, but he didn't wave back. He quickly looked away. Why was he acting shier than usual?

She hadn't heard from StoryTeller2 in a few days. Was he sitting in the audience? Her gaze flew across the gilded seats, looking for boys wearing crowns. She found Daring and his brother, Dexter. Hopper was seated in the third row. Another crown caught her eye, but then the curtains closed, blocking her view. Someone tapped on her arm. She turned around. It was Melody. "Okay, it's our turn. We have a surprise for you."

What did Melody mean? But before Meeshell could ask, a rumbling sound arose. Two giants pushed an enormous aquarium onto the stage. Meeshell looked at Melody with confusion. "It's for you," Melody said with a laugh. "So you can be your true self." Then she turned to her choir. "Follow me. And everyone, break a leg. Or a tail."

The Happily-Glees followed their director onto the stage. Meeshell wasn't sure what to do, but then one of the giants offered her his enormous hand. She stepped into it and was lifted to the water's surface. She dived in, instantly changing into her mermaid self. Most of the students hadn't yet seen her in this form. Even though she was in the water, the one place where she felt most at home, her heart pounded with nervousness. Would this go okay? "Everyone ready?" Melody asked. The choir nodded. The curtains opened and the audience gasped in unison at the vision that greeted them.

Floating with her head above water, Meeshell began to sing. Very few in attendance had ever heard mermaid singing, and once heard, they would never forget. So lovely was the sound, so enchanting, if asked later, no one would truly be able to find words to describe it.

She sang, *"This feeling inside is coming alive. No more waiting now..."* And then, with a kick of her tail, she sailed into the air, did a graceful flip, and landed on two feet. She was wearing her favorite dress, the one with the scalloped coral top and teal skirt, the ruffles moving as gracefully as waves. Beneath the stage lights, her princess mermaid bracelet glittered on her arm, and her white pearlized shoes sparkled. Everyone went wild, cheering and clapping for the performance. Meeshell joined her fellow Happily-Glees in the chorus.

> *"See the fire in our eyes, it's burning brighter.*
> *Let go of the fear and fly, higher and higher.*
> *Rise up, the sky's the limit now, at Ever After High.*
> *Oh oh oh oh oh oh oh!*
> *Power princess shining bright!"*

"They loved you," Melody told Meeshell as loud applause filled the Charmitorium.

"They loved *us*," Meeshell said.

"That was wonderlicious!" Maddie hurried onto the stage. "I guess it's my turn now. Damsels and gentlemen, prepare to be spellbound and behold, as I turn this aquarium into the biggest cup of tea ever after!"

As Maddie worked her magic trick, Headmaster Grimm greeted the choir backstage. "Ms. Piper." He spoke in his usual serious tone.

"Yes, Headmaster?"

"I wanted to inform you that I was delighted by the performance. I didn't feel the need to plug my ears this time."

"Thanks," Melody said.

"And it is nice to see that you are no longer living incognito," he told Meeshell. "Mrs. Trollworth won't be happy with the additional paperwork required to make the change to your name, but the truth is, trolls are rarely happy."

Meeshell made a mental note to take Mrs. Trollworth a bouquet of flowers. Or perhaps, something more troll-worthy, like a jar of bugs.

Apple and Briar were weaving their way through the crowd. "Ms. Beauty!" Headmaster Grimm called. Briar and Apple squeezed between some students who were congratulating Melody.

"Yes, Headmaster Grimm," Briar said.

"A new student will arrive tomorrow morning, from Wonderland. As the head of the Welcoming Committee, I will need you to meet that student at the wishing well portal."

Briar pulled out her MirrorPad and checked her calendar. "I'd be happy to do that, Headmaster, but I have a Party Planning Committee meeting first thing in the morning. However..." Following a long yawn, she tucked the MirrorPad into her bag, then pulled a small badge from her pocket. "I happen to have a new member on the Welcoming Committee who will handle the welcome duties spelltacularly." She pinned the Welcoming Committee badge to Apple's dress. Apple beamed.

A while later, after most of the students had congratulated Melody and her choir, Meeshell, Apple,

Briar, Ashlynn, and Maddie all decided to walk to the village to get mocha lattes. For the first time since getting two legs, there was a lightness to Meeshell's step, a buoyancy to her stride as if she were bobbing on water. She felt authentically happy.

"Now that we know you're not afraid of water, how about going to Mirror Beach this weekend?" Apple asked.

"Yes, you can teach us all how to surf," Briar said.

"That would be fun," Meeshell told them. As they sat at a table beneath a giant oak, waiting for their lattes, Meeshell wanted to send StoryTeller2 a note. Maybe he'd meet her at the beach? But when she pulled out her MirrorPad, she found an urgent message. And it wasn't from StoryTeller2.

Urgent message from Professor Yaga.
We have another injured creature and I could use your help.

Swimming

Lessons

$\mathscr{M}$eeshell and her friends hurried toward the Creature Care Center, but then Meeshell spotted the colorful shape of someone sitting on the beach. It was Professor Yaga. As they grew closer, Meeshell could see that Hunter was there as well. The tide was low, and a series of tide pools had formed. Professor Yaga motioned from the largest tide pool. The girls gathered 'round.

"What's that?" Briar asked, pointing to a black shape lying on the bottom of the pool.

"It's a manta ray," Meeshell explained. She recognized the creature as one of the mantas that she'd ridden many times back home. She knelt on a rock to get a closer look. The manta was listless, his eyes closed.

"This creature is obviously suffering," Professor Yaga said as sunlight bounced off her hoop earrings. "Hunter called me and I got down here as fast as I could, but I cannot figure out how to help him. Can you speak to him?"

"Yes," Meeshell said. "Manta Ray was one of the first languages I learned."

"Oh, can I listen?" Ashlynn said, joining Meeshell. "I'd love to hear what Manta Ray sounds like."

"Sure." Meeshell stuck her head in the water and, to her surprise, Ashlynn stuck hers in as well. Then, with delicate precision, Meeshell blew some bubbles, their sequence spelling out words. The manta opened his eyes and bubbled back. After a few lines of conversation, Meeshell and Ashlynn both sat up and took deep breaths.

"He can't swim," Meeshell reported. "He collided with a shark."

Professor Yaga stuck a gnarled finger into the tide pool and gently stroked the manta ray's back. "If he can't swim, how did he get here?"

"Coral brought him," Meeshell explained.

"Who's Coral?" Apple asked.

"She's the daughter of the Sea Witch," Professor Yaga said. She looked out at the ocean. "Is she still here? It would be helpful to speak with her."

Meeshell expected to hear gasps of surprise at the mention of the Sea Witch, but none of the girls even batted a lash. Hunter looked unfazed as well. Guess they were used to witches of all sorts.

Meeshell pushed her wet hair from her face, then walked from the tide pool to the water's edge. "Coral!" she called, cupping her hands around her mouth. "It's okay. You can show yourself. We want to talk to you!"

Some ripples appeared at the surface. Then a

blue face popped out of the water. "Hello," Coral said to Meeshell.

"Hi," Meeshell said. "Everyone, this is Coral." She introduced the professor and her friends. Apple was the most delighted to meet someone new.

"You're almost old enough to come to Ever After High," Apple said. "Briar and I will make sure you get a warm welcome." She pointed to her Welcoming Committee badge.

"Thanks," Coral told her, smiling shyly.

"What can you tell us about the manta ray?" Professor Yaga asked.

Coral pushed her blue-black hair behind her shoulders and swam closer. "He and a shark got into an argument. I'm not exactly sure what it was about, but you know how opinionated sharks are. Anyway, he ended up getting hurt and he's having trouble swimming. I don't have all my magical powers yet, so I can't magically fix him. I thought someone here could help."

With the professor's guidance, Meeshell, Hunter, and Ashlynn put the manta ray into a tub. Then the girls and Hunter carried the heavy creature over to the Creature Care Center, leaving Coral and Meeshell alone on the beach.

"How are things going?" Coral asked. "I see your legs didn't fall off."

"Yeah, they've been pretty good legs. Thank you for that."

Coral pulled herself onto the beach. She stretched her red tail. "Do you think you'll be okay with living on land? With losing your singing voice?"

Meeshell sat next to her, cross-legged. "I was worried about what I'd do with myself on land, you know, if I couldn't sing and if I couldn't have a tail. But I think I figured it out." She looked up at the care center building. "I will never lose my connection to the sea because I'm going to focus on my studies in Beast Care and Magicment. I'm going to dedicate my life to taking care of sea creatures."

Coral smiled. "Whoa, that's amazing, because I've decided to do the same thing."

"Really?"

"Yeah. When Mom leaves to become a famous singer, I'm going to use my powers as the Sea Witch to take care of creatures, too. So we can work together!" They both laughed. Who could have imagined such a twist to their stories?

"I brought you a surprise." Coral reached into the water and pulled out...

"Finbert!" Meeshell cried. Her little narwhal stuck his happy face out of the water.

"I've been working on a new spell. It's a way for Finbert to stay with you at school. Watch." With a flick of her abalone wand, a little protective bubble formed around Finbert and he floated into the air. With his tail acting like a propeller, he floated straight into Meeshell's outstretched arms.

"This is so amazing," Meeshell said with a laugh. "Thank you!"

After they said good-bye, Coral swam out of the harbor, smacking her red tail one last time before she disappeared beneath the waves. "I'm so glad you're here," Meeshell told her beloved pet. "Wait until you meet my friends. They're going to love you!" She was about to walk up to the Creature Care Center when some splashing sounds drew her attention. It wasn't ordinary splashing, like a fish enjoying some sunbeams, or a seagull diving for a treat. The splashing was urgent and frantic. "Uh-oh," she said to Finbert. "Let's go!"

She ran past the tide pools, around the bluff, and onto Mirror Beach. The beach was empty. An OFF DUTY sign hung from the lifeguard chair. But there, in the water, arms flailed. Someone was trying desperately to stay afloat. Meeshell caught a glimpse of a gold crown and realized instantly who it was.

Then he disappeared under the water.

She was at his side in a heartbeat, pulling him onto shore. He broke into a coughing fit, but she wasn't worried. She knew he'd be fine. He'd only gone under for a moment. "Humphrey, I don't mind saving you, but what if I hadn't come by? Trying to teach yourself to swim with no lifeguard on duty, and no one around to look out for you just isn't a good idea," she told him. She reached out and grabbed his crown before it floated away.

"I can..." He puffed out his chest. "I can..." Then he deflated. "Yeah, you're right. I can't swim."

His floaties lay up the beach, next to a log where he'd left them. She shook her head. "That's not such a big deal! I'm sure a lot of land-dwellers can't swim. Why do you keep risking your life like this?"

"I..." He swallowed hard and looked away. "I thought I needed to swim, so you'd like me."

"Huh?"

Humphrey pulled his legs close and wrapped his arms around them. "I thought you'd only like me if I could swim. You know, because you're a mermaid. I knew you were a mermaid from the first moment I met you." He continued to look away.

"Really?" She was very surprised. "But how could you know that?"

He dug his toes into the sand. "Well, I knew you'd arrived by boat, so that was the first clue. Then I heard you tell Hagatha that you wouldn't eat fish. Second clue. And I saw you jump back from the spilled tea and I realized that you were avoiding water. It all made sense."

Wow, he was as smart as everyone said. "But if you knew I was a mermaid..." He still wouldn't look directly at her. What was he hiding? She knew his big secret, that he couldn't swim, but was there something else? The gleam from his golden crown drew her attention. "Barnacles! Are you Story-Teller2?"

He nodded, and finally looked into her eyes. She couldn't believe it. The secret prince who'd meant so much to her during this first week at school, the prince who'd understood all her doubts and fears and her longing to fit in, had been right in front of

her the whole time. "You've been risking your life for me?"

"Well, yes. I wanted you to like me, but I've never been able to swim. How can a guy like me even hope to get a date with you without being able to swim?"

"Humphrey, you don't need to change yourself for me. Or for anyone. If I'm going to like you, then I have to like you for who you truly are." She stuck his crown on his head. "Besides, I can give you swimming lessons anytime you want."

He suddenly looked terrified.

"Or not," she said. "It's not necessary. Really. It's your choice."

He let out a sigh of relief. "Then...then maybe we can go see a movie at the multihex sometime?"

"Sure," she said happily. "That sounds like fun. But not a shark movie! Those are way too scary!" They both laughed. Then Finbert swam around Humphrey's head, startling him.

"Whoa! A miniature floating narwhal. You don't see that every day."

As soon as her tail had dried, Meeshell and Humphrey headed to the aquarium to join the others. "I meant to tell you...your performance in the Happily-Glees was astounding. I'm glad you found a club."

"Thanks. And I meant to tell you...Thank you for being there, when I needed someone to talk to." She leaned close and gave him a quick peck on his cheek. His entire face turned as red as Coral's tail.

A pair of gulls flew overhead, swooping in lazy circles. A seal barked in the distance, singing its own song. A tiny narwhal swam through the air. Meeshell inhaled the salty scent and smiled. Her heart was full. For she knew, without a doubt, that being her true self was the right thing to be.

And she put one foot in front of the other, taking the steps toward her next adventure.

Acknowledgments

Once again, I am indebted to an amazing team of creative people, without whom this book would simply not be. In Gotham City, you will find my editor Kara Sargent, who guides and protects me, my brilliant copyeditor Christine Ma, publicist extraordinaire Kristina Pisciotto, and many more people, all an important part of the effort, listed here in no particular order (drumroll please): Mara Lander, Véronique Lefèvre Sweet, Lindsay Walter-Greaney, Christina Quintero, Ronnie Ambrose, Dani Valladares, and Victoria Stapleton.

To the creative team at Mattel: Thanks so much to Venetia Davie, Julia Phelps, Ryan Ferguson, Charnita Belcher, Nicole Corse, Darren Sander, Emily Kelly, MJ Offen, Sally Eagle, Lara Dalian, Talia Rodgers, Audu Paden, and Robert Rudman for helping me find my way in their amazing world.

Michael, you deserve a throne.

Bob, Walker, and Isabelle, as always, you are my Happily Ever Afters.

About the Author

$\mathcal{S}$uzanne Selfors feels like a Royal on some days and a Rebel on others. She's written many books for kids, including the Smells Like Dog series and the Imaginary Veterinary series.

She has two charming children and lives in a magical island kingdom, where she hopes it is her destiny to write stories forever after.